Ghastly Gastronomy

Edited by Erin Reynolds

Madness Heart Press
2006 Idlewilde Run Dr.
Austin, Texas 78744

Edited by Erin Reynolds
Cover by John Baltisberger
Interior Layout by Lori Michelle
    www.TheAuthorsAlley.com

First Edition

www.madnessheart.press

Table of Contents

Bearing Fruit

Michael Allen Rose

It appeared to be an ordinary orange. By all accounts, a normal piece of fruit, about four inches in diameter. The light glinted off its shiny exterior.

Gladys was certainly not paranoid. Her friends considered her to be fairly dull and uninteresting, but she could hold her own in a game of bridge, at least. Strangers passed her by without a second glance or, quite often, a first. She was a faceless nobody, and being quite comfortable with that fact, she had no reason to be fearful of anyone or anything. Who would want to kidnap or harm old Gladys?

She had inherited her pragmatism from her mother. Superstition had never been anything but sheer nonsense to her. Perhaps that's why she nearly dropped her dozen eggs when she thought she saw it move. The glint had shifted noticeably in her peripheral vision.

"Clarice?"

A purring lump butted her ankle.

"Clarice, you naughty kitty, were you up on the counter?"

The small calico cat stared in perplexed bewilderment at Gladys.

"Meow?"

"Naughty kitty."

Gladys gave Clarice a light pat on the rump, which sent the cat off to find more appropriate activities than batting fruit about. She turned to put the orange in the crisper.

"Now that's peculiar. Oh, I have such naughty kitties."

The orange had found its way to the other side of the toaster.

Gladys picked the orange up, weighing it in her hand, then carried it to the fridge. She deposited the orange in the crisper drawer, where it came to rest beside two apples and a slightly spongy kiwifruit.

"I think I'll call the girls and see if anyone wants to play bridge tonight," stated Gladys, to nobody in particular. One of her cats, a small black one named Sam-I-Am, looked at her quizzically as she shooed him from the phone table. She would call Dorothy. Dorothy was always good for a visit, and she almost always brought cookies. Gladys liked cookies better than oranges.

There was no answer at Dorothy's house. Gladys left a message:

"Dorothy? Hello? . . . Hello? Yes, this is Gladys. I

hope you're doing well. I just wanted to say hello and see if you and the girls would like to play a little tonight. I hope to see you around seven o'clock then. You and the girls. For cards. All right then. Goodbye."

Gladys hung up the phone and began to plan her next move when she heard something from the kitchen that didn't sound like a cat.

"Kitties? What are you doing in there?"

She propelled herself into the kitchen with extraordinary effort and saw that the fridge door hadn't been properly latched. There was brown French mustard all over the tile, filling in the gaps between shards of broken glass.

Gladys muttered to herself some long-forgotten expletive and went to the sink to find a washrag. The orange had somehow rolled into the sink.

"What a mess. Fruit and condiments everywhere," said Gladys as she began to scoop the glass up into a small paper bag she kept under the sink for just such an occasion. It was at that moment that it occurred to her how difficult it would be for fruit to defy gravity and travel up to a counter-top from behind a closed drawer door. She pondered this.

Dorothy had been weeding her garden, just as she did every day at three o'clock. You don't get the title "Best Garden in the Neighborhood" five years in a row without some blood, sweat, and tears: That's what she always said. She was turning on the sprinklers when she heard the phone ring from inside the house. Her husband, Howard, was out golfing, and even if he had been home, it was unlikely he would have looked up from his newspaper long enough to notice the phone, much less answer its ringing.

She started toward the house, but just then, she spied a thick little vine poking up through the soil right underneath her Juneberry bushes. This would not do. Dorothy quickly forgot about the phone and pulled up her work gloves with a grimace. This was going to get messy.

After a long struggle, Dorothy had successfully extricated the vine from her property and had decided to put the thing to good use. She dropped it on her mulch pile and walked inside the house. While washing her hands with plenty of moisturizer (to keep them from getting all wrinkly from the fertilizers and pesticides), she casually glanced over at the clock. It was a quarter past four. Her gaze moved vertically downward and caught the blinking eye of the answering machine, telling her that she had missed two calls. She casually flicked the "message" button before thoroughly drying and conditioning her hands.

The first message was from the phone company, asking if she wanted to upgrade her service to a new and more exciting plan. She had enough excitement with her Begonias. She waited for the beep signaling the end of the message without paying much attention to the rest of the pitch.

The beep signaling her salvation from the mundane arrived, and she awaited the next message.

"Dorothy? Hello? . . . Hello? Yes, this is Gladys."

Gladys. Wonderful. And she still left her name every time she called. Dorothy had been receiving calls from Gladys for seven years now. She heard that voice in her sleep. Dorothy often woke up with night terrors.

"I hope you're doing well. I just wanted to say hello and see if you and the girls would like to play a little tonight. I hope to see you around seven o'clock then. You and the girls. For cards. All right then. Goodbye."

Dorothy sighed heavily. It wasn't that she disliked Gladys. It's just that Gladys was so . . . well, dull. Gladys needed a hobby so that she could keep herself busy. That's what Dorothy always said, anyway, and nobody seemed to disagree.

After a short but rather intense debate with herself, Dorothy resolved to do her "Christian duty" and made the arrangements with the other girls. Most of them were home, and each had the same reaction: a spilled moment of raw disappointment quickly mopped up by the cloth of civility. Dorothy wasn't sure why Gladys never called the other ladies herself. This has been her cross to bear for most of the years she had known Gladys. Every time there was some kind of social event, like bridge, or quilting circle, or a prayer luncheon, it was Dorothy's unspoken duty to inform the troops.

She laughed at the thought of her circle being "troops" of any kind. The mental image of Gladys firing a Howitzer and being blown backward into a barn made her guffaw until she was embarrassed despite herself, and she sat down to watch some TV before getting ready to go.

At 7:16 PM on the night of Friday the 26th, Sgt. Chuck Derrida got a call at the precinct that sounded something like this:

"Well we're supposed to be playing bridge with our friend Gladys, and all the lights are off, and we just don't know what could be happening in there, because she doesn't drive, and she didn't say her family was coming in or anything, although I keep telling her she should get out more, that's what I always tell her, but now she isn't here, and there's a bunch of ladies freezing outside her house, so if you could send someone by to check on her or something, that would be nice."

Sgt. Derrida told the lady he'd send someone by, just in case she had slipped in the tub or something. This sent the lady on the other end of the line into hysterics. He hadn't had his coffee yet tonight. Derrida could be a real asshole when he hadn't had his coffee.

The ladies were all huddled together, looking through the picture window when officer Brady showed up. They all turned at once, eyes wide open, looking like a gaggle of startled owls. Officer Brady flashed his siren for just a moment, to satisfy his mean-streak, and watched the ladies jump as a unit. He slowly got out of his car and sauntered toward the group.

"It's so dark in there!"

"Can you do something, officer?"

"It's just not like her at all to be all in the dark like that."

He silenced them with a wave of his mighty hand and peered in the window. It was difficult to see anything in the pitch-blackness that the house held captive. He pulled out his flashlight and panned his gaze over the interior of the small home.

Doilies and lace covered everything with a flat surface. There was surprisingly little dust, though, and overall, the place looked fairly tidy. It reminded him of his grandmother's house. There was a small hutch and a cozy-looking chair, left of a door into what looked like a kitchen. He saw a fridge and part of a stove through the door, and then his gaze fell on something rather unexpected.

A single slipper lay there in the doorway. There were stains on it that looked almost black in this light, but he had a suspicion that it was not molasses.

"Just stay calm, ladies. I'm going to call for a detective."

This set off a flurry of concerned questions, none of which he actually heard as he was hurrying back to his squad car. He got on the radio and called for an entry team.

Two hours later, after a long string of protocol-oriented tasks and more than a few rude comments to the ladies, there were detectives flowing freely through the house that Gladys called home. The ladies were very confused, repeatedly commenting that this whole thing was very unlike Gladys. They were also concerned for the cats, which, with all the noise and commotion, were spending quality time under the bed.

Dorothy took a special role in this phase of the operation, stating to the detectives multiple times that the whole thing stank of suspicion. She told them all about the ruffians that hung out at the gas station nearby at night and all the foreigners that had moved into the neighborhood lately. The detectives, although they would have given their right arms to do so, couldn't send the ladies away just yet. These gawking creatures were the closest things to witnesses that were available, so they smiled and nodded when they could bring themselves to do so and ignored them the rest of the time.

The detectives had found no evidence that Gladys had been there, other than the slipper. The stains looked like blood, but it was hard to tell without hearing back from forensics. Some of her groceries had spilled out of the fridge and were presently being put back into the receptacle. The police had taken their pictures, and there was no genuine evidence of foul play, so the head detective decided that it would be best to give the ladies something to do while they combed over the rest of the house.

They had been given explicit orders not to touch or change anything, except the fallen groceries. Once they were done with that, they were supposed to wait to be questioned. Dorothy had heard this order as clearly as anyone, but all the excitement had given her a bit of an upset stomach. Surely, the detective wouldn't mind if she had a little snack. She spied a bright, shiny orange lying on the counter, seemingly untouched, and put it into her bag, quietly.

"How long had you known her? Did she normally go off on vacations without telling anyone? Was this behavior normal for her?"

One by one, the bridge-club told the officers that no, she didn't do this sort of thing, and yes, they were worried, and no they had never heard anything about anyone who she would go to visit without planning first, and no, there were no relatives in the area, and yes, she had called to make plans, and so on. When the detective was largely satisfied that the ladies hadn't made off with poor Gladys, he sent them on their respective ways.

"Where ever could she have gone?" asked Betty, the group's requisite fat member.

The ladies mumbled their own confused replies and slowly began to crawl into their vehicles for a quick departure.

Dorothy walked over to Betty, patted her on the shoulder, and tried to transmit some level of sympathy. Ultimately failing, she got into her car and waved for Betty to get in the passenger side. Betty had been using Dorothy as a taxi service for a number of months now, ever since the day that Betty tried to squeeze behind the wheel of her Geo Metro and found that she could no longer operate a motor vehicle without taking out the front seat completely. Betty enjoyed only one thing more than cooking, and that was eating. She did both of these activities on a regular basis.

Dorothy put the car into gear, and the unlikely pair headed back to Ustwick Heights, the senior-oriented neighborhood in which they shared residence.

"Those boys were so nice to come over and see to Gladys like that," Betty mentioned.

"Well, that's their job, Betty. Like I always say, the taxes pay their salaries, so they'd better do it!"

"Yes, but they were so quick and efficient! It was just exhilarating!" squealed Betty.

The noise of Betty's suppressed giggle made a slight nausea appear in Dorothy's gullet, but she quashed it with a swallow and pretended to be concentrating on the road.

"Do you think I should cook something for them? What do you think police officers like to eat?"

"I'm sure they'd be happy with whatever you made, dear," replied Dorothy, without much thought. Betty's next question was cut off by the abrupt halt of the vehicle. Dorothy pushed the electronic unlock button three times before Betty decided that it was a good time to exit the car. She waved as Dorothy sped around the corner to her own humble home.

Howard's car was in the driveway.

"Hello, dear, I'm home."

Howard brought his paper down below eye level.

"Hello, dear. Where you been? I've been home for an hour."

"I was over at Gladys Haskin's place. She disappeared."

"Oh, really? Some kind of illness?"

"No, she just vanished. Police came and everything."

"No kidding."

"Craziest thing I've ever seen in my life," said

Dorothy as she poured herself some water for tea. "Don't know what might have happened to her. Of course, I've been telling her for years that she should find someone to live with again. Keeps this sort of thing from occurring, in my experience."

"Disappeared, huh?" Harold had gone back inside the wall of his newspaper.

"Right out of her house."

"Hm," he muttered, "what a world. Say, you should have seen the slice I hit on hole three tonight. Stunning! Right on the green in one shot. I birdied without even thinking."

"That's nice, dear," said Dorothy as she sat down in the kitchen to unwind. It had been a very long evening, and now all she wanted to do was enjoy her tea and perhaps something to settle her stomach. All she had eaten all day was a small bowl of beef noodle soup. She remembered the orange that she had taken from Gladys's house and opened her bag.

Howard put his arm on the end table, as he was prone to do while reading his paper. Something nudged his arm.

"Oh, that woman."

He gazed lovingly at the orange that Dorothy laid there for him to enjoy. She was always ragging on him about his Vitamin C intake. This was her subtle way of getting the message across without being a nag. He picked it up and looked at it. It was a good-sized orange, pleasantly plump with a soft but firm peel. It looked delicious. He readied himself to take the first bite.

"Thank you, sweetheart!" he yelled to the kitchen.

Dorothy didn't hear this. She was too busy

wondering what had happened to her purse. The orange was gone, and so was most of her tissue paper. Things were not where she left them, at any rate. She walked to the fridge to see if she had absentmindedly put it away without thinking, but there was nothing there that shouldn't be. Only a small plum and a bag of apples filled the crisper drawer. There was also some prune juice on the top shelf. At Harold's age, he needed to stay regular for good health: That's what she always said.

Harold was making the most godawful chewing noises from the living room.

"Keep it down in there, you sound like a horse!" shouted Dorothy, as she closed the fridge door. Her mother always said she should have married someone who chewed with his mouth closed, but Dorothy hadn't listened. Dorothy couldn't stand people who always gave out advice to others. That's what's wrong with the world. At least, that's what she always told people.

Dorothy sat down to her tea and a gardening magazine and reflected on her life. This went on for a short while until the noises became too much to bear, so she thumped loudly on the wall with a nearby broom.

"Harold, chew politely, please!"

She was met with silence.

"What are you eating in there?" she asked him, her suspicions growing by the minute. "Is that my orange? Well, I hope you've left some for me is all I can say."

Dorothy walked through the door to find an empty chair with a rather clumsily folded newspaper lying in it. Her orange glinted up at her from the end table.

"Harold? Where did you get off to? You'd better not be going out for a beer!"

Wherever he had gone, Harold had, at any rate, left her the orange. At least one thing had gone right this evening. She hurried to the kitchen, orange in hand, to find the peeler.

The "secondary silverware" drawer was a travesty of spatulas, meat prongs, whisks, and grapefruit spoons. Within seconds she had dug through the chaos and found her peeler, a bright plastic thing, molded just sharp enough to peel a citrus fruit, but not to cut hands. She held the orange up to get a better look and moved the peeler closer to the sphere.

"DING-DONG"

"Oh, drat, did he lock himself out of the house again?"

Dorothy forgot her fruit momentarily and went to answer the door. The orange calmly rolled under the spice rack.

Betty was standing there, taking up far too much space for one person, grinning a sugar-soaked, friendly grin. She held a measuring cup in one hand, and the other was coated in flour.

"Dorothy, dear, sorry to disturb you, but I was making up some goodies for the boys in blue and was wondering if I could borrow a few itsy-bitsy things?"

"Fine . . . fine . . . say, you didn't see . . . Harold out there, did you?"

"Harold? No, can't say that I have. You think he went for a walk?"

"He must have," stated Dorothy, trying to convince herself as much as Betty. "Well, he'll be back soon enough, I'm sure. Feel free to borrow whatever you need from the pantry or the kitchen."

"Thank you so much!" came Betty's red-cheeked reply. She waddled her way to the staircase to check in the pantry. "I won't be but a few minutes, I promise!"

With Betty out of the way, Dorothy went to retrieve her orange in peace and quiet. She could swear, with the way the light hit it, the orange almost looked like it was grinning at her.

It was several minutes before Betty came up the stairs, arms laden with sacks of chocolate chips and brown sugar. It didn't take much to make Betty considerably laden, as her arms couldn't effectively reach down to tie her own shoes. She worked her way toward the kitchen, trying not to knock any pictures off the walls with her sizeable frame.

"Dorothy? I was thinking of making something with mixed fruit. Do you have any?"

As she walked into the kitchen, she saw the perfect orange sitting on the table, and quickly snatched it up. She also took the plum and half the bag of apples that were in the fridge.

"Dorothy? Are you sure you don't mind?"

The sound of a ticking clock was all that met her query.

"Dorothy? . . . Well, she must have gone out to find Harold. I hope nothing happens to her. Strange things are out at night." Continuing to mutter herself into a sense of security, she carefully locked the door of her friend's house and shuffled down the street to her own modest home.

Betty's kitchen was her pride and joy. Everywhere in it, little signatures were apparent: from the "Betty's Kitchen" magnet on her fridge to the oven-mitt that she had gotten from her Nephew after he had visited France. It had pictures of the Eiffel Tower all over it. Betty considered this part of her "exotic" collection.

Betty dumped her fruit out on the counter and plugged in her electric knife. She knew what men liked. Men liked good cooking. She never could figure out why she couldn't land a husband. She pondered this as she absentmindedly started eating chocolate chips, straight from the bag.

After she had assembled all her ingredients, she began to mix. Before she forgot, though, this recipe called for real fruit. Without even looking, her expert hands sought out the orange. It was as though her hands had a direct link to the radar that was her stomach. They could find food in a thick fog at midnight. She put the orange down on the cutting board, holding it very tightly so that she didn't cut herself, and began to section it. The orange seemed very calm . . . for an orange.

Brady? There's someone here to see you."

"All right, send her in."

Officer Brady was sitting behind his desk, going over the incident with the old lady. They still hadn't found any sign of her, and they had been searching all night. What bothered him were the weird clues they had found, if you could even call them that. The slipper had come up clean. What they thought had been blood was actually cranberry juice, spilled that evening. Other than that, there were no signs of a struggle, no signs of forced entry . . . nothing. The detectives were stumped. He held his head up to greet a rather large woman who was staring down at him.

"Hello, officer! I'm Betty Kringle. I just wanted to thank you boys for being so helpful last night with poor Gladys disappearing and all that. I baked these for you."

She handed him a box, lovingly tied with a yellow ribbon.

"Why, thank you, Ms. Kringle. I appreciate it, and I'm sure my officers will too."

"You're so welcome. Have you found anything new yet?"

"No ma'am, but we're still looking. Why don't you go home and relax? I'm sure someone will let you know if we find anything."

"Thank you so much, officer. You call me if you need anything! Bye now!" Betty waved and pushed herself through the door. Officer Brady opened the box to see what delights awaited him. They looked absolutely delectable, every one a gem. Little flecks of fruit dotted several of them, and the others were coated with a fine glaze. Everyone would love these. She had made enough for everyone on the force! He left the box to go get his friends from the break room.

Despite the low growling of hunger and the weird glint that made them seem almost predatory, they appeared to be a couple dozen ordinary doughnuts. They tried not to quiver in anticipation.

⫸ **RECIPE** ⫷

Evil Orange Cranberry Dream Cookies

1/2 cup (8 tablespoons) unsalted butter
3/4 cup sugar
Zest of 1 small lemon
Zest of 1 small lime
Zest of 1 medium orange*
1 teaspoon vanilla extract
1/4 teaspoon baking powder
1/2 teaspoon salt
1 large egg
1 1/2 cups All-Purpose Flour
2 cups dried cherry-flavored cranberries

Preheat the oven to 425°F. Lightly grease a large baking sheet.

In a large bowl, beat the butter, sugar, vanilla, baking powder, salt, orange zest lemon zest, and lime zest together.

Beat in the egg.

Add the flour and dried cranberries, stirring until well combined.

Drop the dough by heaping teaspoonfuls onto the baking sheets, leaving about 1 1/2" between them. Dough balls should be about 1 1/4" in diameter. Flatten the cookies slightly, to about 1/2" thick.

Bake the cookies for 6 to 7 minutes, until they're

barely set, and a light golden brown around the edges. Don't over-bake; if you do, the cookies will be hard, not awesome.

Remove the cookies from the oven, and cool them on the pan. If you need a pan to bake the more cookies, give the cookies about 5 minutes to set before transferring them to a rack to cool completely.

* Please use only normal oranges. Do not use evil alien oranges. Evil alien oranges may devour you or your loved ones. Even when disassembled from their original form, evil alien oranges remain extremely dangerous. That's how they propagate their species. Look at the orange you've selected. Is it still where you put it down? Are you sure? Look again. Look closely. I thought it was a few inches to the left, before. Take a very close and careful look, and just be absolutely sure that it appears to be an ordinary orange . . . **

** If the person who was reading this is dead or missing, and all you see is an orange sitting in a pool of blood, resume at step 3 or so.

Everybody Loves Pizza

Karen Heslop

rolled my eyes when I passed four workmen attaching a sign to the old store. **The Pizza Addict**. *I hope it lasts longer than the other 500 businesses that opened in this middle of nowhere town.* It was on my route from work, though, so I was guaranteed to taste the food eventually.

A few days passed before their lights came on, and I got my chance. It was a little after 10 p.m., so the few other shops in the plaza were dark, giving the pizza place more prominence. On the inside, bright yellow lights illuminated one customer and a cashier standing ramrod straight at the register.

As I got to the front door, I saw 'Free Delivery' tacked on to the business sign. *Well, that's presumptuous.* The door swung open easily, and in spite of the lone customer steadily chewing on his pizza, the shop's air was almost sterile. A brunette cashier smiled at me, exposing an uncomfortable number of teeth. The same font from the sign was stencilled into the name pin stuck to her shirt. *Petra.* Her light-grey eyes shone like clouds promising brief showers.

"Good night, sir. Welcome to The Pizza Addict. What would you like to order tonight?"

Sir? I couldn't have been more than seven years older than her. Ten at the most.

"Uhm . . . what's good here?"

She tilted her head as if trying to process my question.

"Everything's good here, sir. Is there anything in particular you usually like on your pizza?"

"Well, I usually go for the all-meat kind, but I've been trying to eat healthier so . . . "

"I understand, sir. You should try our roast chicken veggie pizza."

"OK. I'll try a small one."

"Dine-in or take-out?"

"Dine-in is fine."

"That'll be $6.50. Can I have a name for the bill?"

"James Pinkerton."

I paid, and as I took a seat close to the door, I noticed the other customer had left. His used napkins were crumpled balls scattered across the table. I looked at the cashier, expecting her to pull double duty and clean up. She stared back at me, the same smile stretched across her eager face. I looked away and tried to focus on the rest of the eerily quiet pizzeria. *Shouldn't there be sounds of my pizza being made?*

As soon as the thought crossed my mind, a bell dinged.

"Your order is ready, sir."

Her voice carried clearly across the empty room, and the sound of my footfalls echoed through the shop. A chill prickled my skin. *Maybe I should take my order to go.* My lips parted, but the cashier's unchanged smile held my words. I took my tray and returned to the table.

A yellowish-beige crust mottled with green and brown lumps slumped in the small cardboard box. Wisps of steam curled into the air but carried no aroma. The slice warmed my hand as I took a tentative bite, and I was pleasantly surprised when the intricate flavours danced on my tongue. Mouthfuls of meat and vegetables slid easily into my curious stomach. Before long, my fingers brushed cardboard, and I looked down in confusion. Somehow I had eaten all four slices. At the counter, the cashier's smile adopted a tinge of warmth.

The next day at lunch, I picked at the crust on the canteen's roast chicken sandwich. Usually my favourite, the few morsels I had nibbled on tasted like ash. I gulped down the rest of my grape soda. *I guess it's pizza again later.*

The guy from the night before was there again. Plus a couple new patrons. None of them looked my way when I stepped in. Petra's smile unnerved me less now that I was expecting it. Her voice was deep and familiar as she greeted me.

"Good evening, Mr. Pinkerton. Welcome back to The Pizza Addict. What would you like today?"

"Something with a lot of meat."

"Our meat eaters' special it is then."

"Yes. A small, please."

"Dine-in or take-out?"

"Dine-in."

"That will be $6.50."

I paid and took my seat. Faint noises slipped into the dining area. Thwack. Thud. Squelch? The other patrons chewed their slices. Synchronized. The bell dinged.

"Your order is ready, Mr. Pinkerton."

Eyeing the other patrons, I tried unsuccessfully to chew at a different rhythm. Like clockwork, we all brought the slice to our lips, chewed, chewed, chewed, and swallowed until it was all gone. I was about to throw the box in the trash when a lilting voice surprised me.

"Did you enjoy your pizza, Mr. Pinkerton?"

My eyes flicked from her grey eyes to her name pin. *Fiona.* Petra grinned at me from the front of the store. I turned back to the twin smile before me.

"Y-yes, I did."

I was halfway home before I realized the box was still in my hand. Staunchly opposed to littering, I held it by the tips of my fingers until I was at my neighbourhood garbage skip. My discarded box settled in comfortably with many others like it.

My neighbours really like pizza, huh?

Getting through the next morning at work had been like slogging through thick, congealing mud. I'd only been able to focus on one thing all day.

Pizza.

Now that it was finally lunchtime, I craved nothing but . . .

Pizza.

Except it makes no sense to leave work to get pizza from The Pizza Addict and then come back . . . unless I faked an illness or something.

Delivery.

Right, yes. They deliver.

An Internet search spit out their details quickly. Beads of sweat lined my forehead as the tinny sound of a ringing phone tickled my ear. My fingers tapped a frantic rhythm on the desk.

"The Pizza Addict."

"Uh . . . hi. I would like to order a medium meat lovers' pizza for delivery."

"Of course. May I have your address and phone number, please?"

After receiving the information, the voice on the phone seemed to brighten.

"Ah, Mr. Pinkerton. I'm happy to serve you. Your pizza will be there in 30 minutes or less."

My mouth hung open long after the phone clicked in my ear. Questions clattered around my head until I heard a knock on my door.

"Delivery from The Pizza Addict."

Her eyes were almost colourless when I looked at

her. A smile played on her pale lips. *Petra?* I looked for her name pin. *Davi.* I paid and took my bag. As I bit into the first slice, my co-worker, Theodore, stepped in. A broad grin lit up his face.

"Could that possibly be something other than the generic crap they serve in the cafeteria? How did you get that past Mr. Keyes' prying, judgemental eyes?"

I shrugged.

Go away, Theodore.

"Spot me a piece? I'll get you next time."

No.

"Sure."

My eyes tracked him as he left my office and engaged in casual conversation with another co-worker. He paused to take a bite of the slice and then turned slowly to look at me. We chewed in unison.

I tried to fight the urge. I really did. Theodore was at the usual customer's table when I walked in. His eyes were glossy as he chewed on his pizza. For the first time, there was no representative at the register or anywhere else in the dining area.

Pizza.

I knocked on the counter.

"Hello?"

No answer.

Pizza.

I banged on the counter some more. Nothing. I vaulted over the counter and headed in the direction of the kitchen. As I pushed open the door, a sweet, sickly scent wafted from the inside. Petra was standing in front of the stove, stirring a thick liquid in a large pot. The metallic clang of the spoon hitting the sides of the pot rang through the room. I pushed the door wider so she could see me.

"Excuse me, I . . ."

There was a low keening when I entered the room. A creature the shade of molten lava speckled with fungus-like grey sprouts lay spread-eagled on the ground. Long, skeletal hands cradled an engorged belly that twitched like a garbage bag keeping in agitated maggots. The keening built up to a short screech, but Petra paid the creature no attention. Instead, she turned to me with her unwavering smile.

"Good evening, Mr. Pinkerton. If you don't mind returning to the waiting area, I'll be right with you."

Before I could reply, there was a wet plop letting loose a thick, orange liquid from the creature, followed by a writhing mass of spindly, pale things. Unfazed, Petra cupped her hands around the tiny beings before they could get away and dropped them into a container beside the stove. The oven dinged, and she removed several golden brown pizza crusts. She sprinkled the worms over the crusts, and they burrowed into the bronzed dough like jittery mozzarella shavings. As she ladled sauce from the pot into the crusts, my daze broke, and I stumbled from the kitchen.

A film of cold sweat coated my face when I reached the counter. A waiting customer stared at me expectantly while wringing her hands.

"Do you work here? I need to place an order."

"No . . . I . . . excuse me."

She made way as I fumbled over the counter. Words of warning threatened to vomit up from my belly, but I couldn't bring myself to speak. Suddenly, it seemed less urgent.

"Mr. Pinkerton?"

I turned to find Petra standing there. Smiling, always smiling. She handed me a bag.

"Your order is ready."

"But, I didn't . . ."

"For your trouble."

Pizza.

"Yes."

I returned to my seat and ate. The flavours were new. I would have to ask her what this one was next time I came in.

The next morning, my fingers cramped as I struggled to button my pants. I tried to suck in the paunch I had developed, but it wouldn't budge. With tentative pokes, I probed the girth of my stomach. The skin was rubbery and almost numb. It took me a moment to realize my feathery touches were only registering in my fingertips and not the skin I was touching.

Curious, I pressed harder. The flesh squished and squelched beneath my hands. It was . . . malleable.

What the hell?

I considered staying home, but Mr. Keyes was already suspicious of the sick day I took last week.

Well, if it can be moved . . .

I grabbed a handful of the flesh I couldn't feel and

moulded it into a shape my pants could button over. I completed my outfit with an oversized jersey and headed out. My feet dragged as I plodded along my usual route. The sparkly yellow sign called to me from across the road.

I should go to work. I need to go to work.

My stomach grumbled in reply, all hunger and mushy flesh. I shook my head and crossed the road.

I can't work on an empty stomach.

I trudged home on listless legs, my growing stomach straining against its constraints. My intestines were twisting around on themselves, creeping towards my spine like rats fleeing a fire. I staggered to the bathroom with my palm clamped over my mouth. Once at the sink, orange liquid poured from my mouth, tinged with the sickly stench of rot.

There was a tentative knock on my door. I looked at the strange liquid in the sink again before washing it away.

Knock, knock, knock.

"I'm coming."

I wasn't expecting anyone, so I kept the chain latched while inching the door open. Pale grey eyes and a broad smile greeted me.

Petra?

A cursory glance at the name tag confirmed it.

"Hello, Mr. Pinkerton. I believe I can be of some assistance."

"With what? I didn't call you . . . "

She tilted her head at my stomach, and pain seared through me as if on cue. I unlatched the door and waddled over to my couch. She followed with a small, black case in hand.

"What are you . . . ?"

"I must get our young."

Their young?

My stomach muscles clenched again, and I groaned. Petra's cool hands were under my shirt, poking and prodding. A pencil-length metal device was clenched between her thin, unlined lips. She gave a satisfied sigh as she found what she was searching for. She took the device from her lips and tinkered with it until there was a flashing green light. Her lips curled into the usual smile.

"Please hold still, Mr. Pinkerton."

She plunged a needle into my side, and numbness seeped into my torso. She used a laser to cut away the circle of skin covering the span between my ribcage and pelvic bone. I gagged on the miasma of singed skin and flesh. Gently, she lifted the mass away, and my eyes widened. There were five thick larval shapes the size of my fist nestled into the flesh. I peered down at myself. A thin transparent veil kept my inner organs inside, but there was a crater where my enlarged stomach used to be.

"What did you do?"

Ignoring me, Petra guided each one out onto the floor. The writhing pale-yellow worms fit snugly in the palm of her hand. As I watched, six long, spindly appendages sprung from each creature, and they tottered on my frayed carpet. She smiled softly when they started mewling. The mewling was almost like newborn kittens. Almost.

"Take it easy little ones. This planet isn't quite ours yet."

She opened the door, and they skittered outside. For the first time, I noticed the van in my driveway. Petra waved at me as she pulled the van's door open, and the creatures clambered in. I lost count of the other pairs of antennae in the vehicle. With her signature smile in place, Petra turned to me.

"They are always so eager to get about—the young ones. It must be why the Ambassador sent us ahead of everyone else."

My mind whirled.

Everyone else?

Before I could ask any questions, she placed a bag emblazoned with The Pizza Addict logo beside me. I stared at her numbly.

"For your trouble."

My mind calmed as my fingers crept towards the bag. I turned the television on and ate my pizza as the newsman droned on about the day's activities. Feeling crept back into my body as I chewed, and my stomach returned to normal.

The monotony of the news was broken by a vivid, lime-yellow advertisement.

The Pizza Addict. Stores now opening across the state! Come feed your inner addict!

Good for them, a lot of people like pizza.

➤➤➤ **RECIPE** ◀◀◀

Roast Chicken Veggie Pizza

Chicken
- 1 Chicken
- ¾ cup butter (melted)
- 1 tbsp Salt
- 1 tbsp Papricka
- 1/4 tbsp black pepper

Crust
- 1 package (1/4 ounce) active dry yeast
- 1 cup warm water (110° to 115°)
- 2 tbsp canola oil
- 1 tsp salt
- 1 tsp sugar
- 2-3/4 to 3-1/4 cups all-purpose flour

Sauce:
- 1 can (15 ounces) tomato sauce
- 1 small onion, chopped
- 3/4 tsp Italian seasoning
- 1/4 tsp garlic powder
- 1/4 tsp salt
- 1/8 tsp pepper
- 1 cup Broccoli florets
- 1/2 cup shiitake mushrooms sliced
- 2 cups shredded mozzarella

Cook the Chicken

Season the inside of the chicken with a pinch of salt. Place the chicken onto a rotisserie and set the grill on high. Cook for 10 minutes.

During that time, quickly mix together the butter, 1 tablespoon of salt, paprika and pepper. Turn the grill down to medium and baste the chicken with the butter mixture. Close the lid and cook for 1 to 1 1/2 hours, basting occasionally, until the internal temperature reaches 180°F (83°C) when taken in the thigh with a meat thermometer.

Remove from the rotisserie and let stand for 10 to 15 minutes before cutting into piece, set aside

Cook the Pizza

Preheat oven to 375°F. In a large bowl, dissolve yeast in warm water. Add the oil, salt, sugar and 2 cups flour. Beat on medium speed for 3 minutes. Stir in enough remaining flour to form a soft dough.

Turn onto a floured surface; knead until smooth and elastic, 6-8 minutes. Place in a greased bowl, turning once to grease top. Cover and let rest in a warm place for 10 minutes.

Meanwhile, combine sauce ingredients; set aside. Divide dough in half. On a floured surface, roll each portion into a 13-in. circle. Transfer to greased 12-in. pizza pans; build up edges slightly. Prick dough thoroughly with a fork.

Bake until lightly browned, 12-15 minutes. Spread sauce over hot crusts to within 2-in. of edges; top with chicken, mushrooms, broccoli and cheese. Bake 20 minutes longer or until cheese is melted.

Sweet Tooth

Joel Murray

The faceless thing carried the old woman's body into the closet and deposited it there. The thing had no need for her flesh. Her home, on the other hand, a vine-clutched mansion in the center of town, elaborately decorated for Halloween, was another matter. Carved, candle-filled pumpkins lined the porch. Sheet ghosts haunted every window. Plastic skeletons hung jangling in the wind. A festive beacon aglow in the blustery fall night.

The faceless thing pulled its mask down to hide its hideous visage. Its false face, orange plastic, grinned and winked deviously. A jack-o'-lantern.

The faceless thing, faceless no more, stirred a slender, crooked finger in the candy bowl. The bowl was smooth black, full to the brim. The plastic wrappers whispered conspiratorially against the thing's ancient skin. Its secret recipe.

The doorbell rang, and a chorus of child voices yelled, "TRICK OR TREAT!" in wild unison. The faceless thing turned to answer their call, and Halloween night began.

"Milk Duds for your Reese's?"

"Sure. Hate how those stick to my teeth."

"Score." The candy changed gloved hands. "How about your Mike and Ikes? My mom loves those."

"Yuck. Swap 'em for your Nerds?"

"Okay."

June dropped the Mike and Ikes into her pillowcase and peered intently into the riot of colorful wrappers. Her haul would make Mom and Dad grin, she knew. She'd been careful to collect mostly their favorites: Mike and Ikes and Almond Joys for Mom, Snickers and Three Musketeers for Dad. She'd amassed a small collection of peanut butter cups too; Reese's were her personal favorite.

June was crazy for peanut butter. It was one of the only treats that wouldn't spike her blood sugar. She'd eat big spoonfuls of it for dessert almost every night.

"I swear, June-bug, one of these days you're gonna turn into a peanut," her Dad would say, smiling. "And then I'll have to butter you up and eat ya!" Then her old man would plant a big scratchy-mustache kiss on her forehead, and June would roll her eyes and scoop another spoonful from the jar.

Peanut butter *cups*, on the other hand, weren't an everyday treat for June, but they did come in handy for lows. Nine grams of carbohydrates straight to the ol' bloodstream. She always had a couple on hand, just in case her glucose dropped. She was sensitive to her insulin shots, delivered into her thin layer of belly fat with each meal; the dose varied depending on how many carbohydrates the meal contained. She'd be running around the neighborhood after lunch or walking around the mall with Mom, so caught up in playing or shopping or whatever that seemingly out of the blue she'd realize her hands were shaking, her heart racing like a jackrabbit's, head all dizzy. Times like that, eating a Reese's was more than a treat to June. It was a lifesaver.

"Trade ya my Lifesavers for your Jolly Ranchers?" Sam proposed.

"Aw, you can just have 'em," June replied.

Sam's eyebrows rose. "You sure?"

"Sure thing. No biggie," June grinned. "You know I'm into trick or treating for the tricks mostly."

The pair were sitting on June's porch, flanked by one wickedly grinning jack-o'-lantern, Mom's handiwork, and another grimacing pumpkin, vomiting pumpkin seeds and orange goop down the steps, Dad's handiwork. The sweet scent of burning pumpkin filled their nostrils as they bartered.

Halloween was almost over, and June wished it didn't have to end. While it seemed a cruel trick that she couldn't indulge in treats like her friends did—Sam had already consumed around half his gathered loot—the holiday was still June's absolute favorite. This year she was a vampire. Plastic fangs, lipstick blood.

June passed Sam the candy. Sam was a goblin. His green mask was pushed up, maniacally grinning skyward. He took the candy and smiled at June appreciatively. Only your very best friends just *gave* you their Halloween candy, diabetic or not. June was Sam's bestest and oldest, hands down.

"Thanks, June." He deposited the Jolly Ranchers in his plastic pumpkin and continued rifling through its contents. After a moment, a quizzical look dawned on his face. "Hey, ya ever seen a Choc-o'-Lantern before?" June leaned over to peer at the orange-wrappered candy Sam held out to her. A winking pumpkin design peered back through one glowing eye. "Any idea what kinda candy it is?"

"Uh-uh," June shook her head. "Maybe it's new?"

"Maybe. Worth a try, I guess." Sam unwrapped it, revealing a pumpkin-shaped lump of chocolate with the same winking expression stamped into its surface. Sam took a bite, examining the now-exposed innards of the remaining candy as he chewed.

"Hm, not bad. Wanna try?" His eyebrows raised, he held the second half of the Choc-o'-Lantern out to June.

"No, thanks," she replied, feeling her holiday high spirits deflate a little. She knew Sam was being nice, but refusing offered sweets was a familiar annoyance to June. Of course, he remembered her diabetes—she'd had the disease their entire friendship—but it still dredged up echoes of awkwardness past.

When teachers brought the class treats, like the monkey munch Ms. Landy distributed before the Halloween parade last week, or when kids brought cupcakes or brownies or whatever to share with everyone for their birthdays, June would usually politely refuse. It was simpler not to partake, to avoid her sugar potentially shooting into the stratosphere, making her feel bleary and lethargic, to avoid potentially overcorrecting with an insulin shot, sending her low and leaving her feeling *really* awful.

Simpler to refuse, yes. But almost always uncomfortable. June was sensitive to the friction her refusal caused, the mild grind of her gear against normal middle school social expectations. Kids *wanted* sweets. There was that expression: *like a kid in a candy shop*. A kid with a sweet tooth embodied the natural order, an unwritten rule of childhood whose violation raised eyebrows. The occasional compulsion for the treat offerer to push the issue— "Are you sure you don't want one, honey?"—drove June a little nuts too. She even suspected, with a whiff of cynicism beyond her years, the insistence belied the fact that treat sharing wasn't really "being nice" at all, but a social transaction paying back no dividends from June and her broken pancreas. Ugh. Feeling pressured to justify her refusal by explaining her disease made June feel even more abnormal. She didn't want pity or attention.

Sam shrugged and popped the other half of the Choc-o'-Lantern into his mouth.

At that moment, a husky werewolf riding a bike drifted by on the sidewalk in front of June's house, followed by a lanky ghost riding a scooter, sheet flapping behind it. The werewolf's backpack was full of toilet paper rolls and egg cartons.

"Hey look, it's fatso and the needle queen," the werewolf sneered, pulling its bike to a stop in front of the porch. "Stuffing your fat face some more, huh, fatso? Halloween must be heaven for you."

The ghost giggled. Sam, his mouth full, turned red.

"Really? Aren't you a little old to be picking on seventh graders?" June shot back. "*Very* macho. Get off my lawn."

"What are you gonna do about it, needle queen? Suck my blood? I'll give you something else to suck on. The ghost chortled again, and the pair high-fived.

"You wish." June rolled her eyes. "How about I stab you with one of my needles at lunch next week, when you're not expecting it? See how much blood I can draw?" June's pen needles didn't work that way—they pumped insulin and didn't suck anything—but these idiots were way too stupid to know anything about her diabetes equipment. "How about I go get one right now?"

She stood up, took a step toward the bullies.

The werewolf took a step backward. "Jeezus, calm down, psycho. We're just joking. You're a sick puppy, you know that?" It remounted the bicycle. "See you losers in hell!"

The ghost chuckled and pedaled after, leaving June and Sam alone once more.

"Assholes," June muttered.

Sam stared at his feet. He was sensitive about his weight, and June felt her anger flare at the bullies for putting a damper on their Halloween fun.

"So, what was in it?" June asked. "Any good?"

"In what?"

"The Choc-o'-Lantern, duh."

"Oh." Sam perked up a bit. "I'd give it an eight outta ten. Some kinda caramel, nougaty filling. Little pieces of something in it. Peanuts maybe?" He noticed a bit of chocolate residue left on his fingers, licked it off.

June raised an eyebrow. Sometimes hearing food described was nearly as good as tasting it herself. It sounded right up Dad's alley. "Got any more?"

"Yep." Sam reached into his bag.

"Trade ya?"

"Just take it, June. For the Jolly Ranchers. And for being the best." Sam smiled and blushed a little. He held out a pair of Choc-o'-Lanterns.

June smiled back and took the proffered sweets. "Aw, shucks. Thanks, Sammo."

Mom poked her head out the screen door. Time for bed, June-bug.

"Okay, Mom." The kids rose from the stoop, stretched. "See ya tomorrow, Sam." With swift dexterity, the pair knocked fists, which exploded on contact. Their wiggling fingers performed an intricate dance, and they slapped palms up, down, and sideways. The secret handshake was as old as their friendship and deeply ingrained in muscle memory.

"Catch ya later, *June-bug*." Sam sprung up, candy in hand, giggling. His usage of the embarrassing pet name couldn't go unanswered. With a ghastly undead hiss, June bared her plastic fangs and chased Sam off the porch, her clawed hands reaching for him. Sam scampered away, still chortling with laughter.

"Happy Halloween, June!"

She grinned. "Happy Halloween, Sammo!"

She watched him go, weaving between the plastic gravestones and clutching skeleton hands protruding from the front yard, swinging his pumpkin pail as he looked both ways and crossed the street, until he slipped through the front door of his house and disappeared inside.

June sighed and surveyed her neighborhood. Orange and purple lights strung through cobwebbed trees and bushes and along rooftops blinked and glowed. Moonlight reflected off plastic skulls and spiders and severed limbs. Spook men, wearing flannels and jeans and last year's masks stuffed with newspaper, slumped menacingly on porch chairs. Laughter hooted distantly, and tires squealed. A cloud engulfed the moon, and June shivered, goosebumps pimpling her arms. She looked up, watched bats flit around the eaves, and breathed deep the crisp autumn night air. Closing her eyes, June marinated one last moment in the holiday. With another sigh, she turned and headed back inside.

June awoke from a familiar dream to a thump at the front door. Her head fuzzy, she groped her glucose meter from the nightstand, pierced her left index finger with a lancet, and squeezed a drop of red onto the test strip. "Like milking a cow," the nurse instructor had explained in June's first endocrinologist appointment after her diagnosis. She never could shake that unsettling metaphor.

"138," the meter glowed at her. *Phew.*

Shoulda made a tiny vampire costume for my glucose meter, June mused, rubbing her eyes. All the blood I feed the little fella.

Another thump at the front door. June glanced at her phone. 3:19 AM. Halloween was officially over. Beyond late for trick-or-treaters, pushing it for the toilet-paper-and-egg-slinging older kids even.

Despite the strange thumping, June felt relief at the banishment of the dream. It was a variation on a familiar theme: her blood sugar low, *very* low—in the 40s—stuck somewhere without food or her testing supplies, this time in a strange deserted neighborhood. Her hands shaking, her heart galloping, her vampire costume soaked in sweat. If she dropped below 30, she could have seizures, lose consciousness, die. She ran from door to door, screaming, "TRICK OR TREAT!" but nobody came. Nobody offered a sweet that could save her—no Reese's, no Snickers, no Choc-o'-Lanterns. Only the silent glow of carved pumpkins, offering nothing but their mindless grins, mocking her panic.

She always tested when she woke up from dreams like this. Better safe than sorry. She was well in the safe zone, and the relief was blissful.

A muffled voice croaked something unintelligible from the porch, and another thump shook the doorframe.

"Sam?" June whispered and slipped out of bed. It sounded like him, but weird somehow. Like he had a bad head cold, mucus in the throat.

June tiptoed downstairs. What could Sam want? Maybe he was sleepwalking? Something about Sam's voice made June crack the door and peer out, instead of swinging it open as she normally would.

Sam was standing on the porch, swaying gently. Behind him, a riot of crimson leaves danced across the lawn. Sam's eyes were glazed, his breathing labored. He sucked big gulps of air with each wheezing breath. A vein stood out in his forehead. He was wearing Halloween pajamas, patterned festively in orange pumpkins and black bats. A trickle of drool hung from his bottom lip.

"Sam, what are you doing? What's wrong?" June hissed.

"June . . ." Sam moaned and clutched his stomach. "Please help . . . my stomach . . . my throat . . . " His voice was lower than usual, froggy. He began to lurch toward her, then stopped, doubled over in pain.

"Sam, where are your parents?" She opened the door and stepped toward him.

"They never came home . . . from their Halloween party," Sam croaked weakly. He looked terrible, sweat-soaked.

June took another step toward him, reached her hand out.

With a horrible choking groan, Sam vomited. June closed her eyes in a grimace and stepped back, waiting to hear it splatter on the porch. Throw-up sounds were the worst.

The splatter didn't come. Her eyes opened and widened in horror.

A pendulum of chunky brown and sickly greenish upchuck hung from Sam's open mouth, his throat clogged with it, his jaw straining open to its widest limit. His choking sobs were muffled by the disgusting tentacle of half-digested candy, which was moving, gently swaying like a cobra to a flutist's melody. Pressed against the door, frozen in terror, June watched the vomit tentacle curl upwards, a flexing arm of chocolate bile. As it rose, its fist paused, wavered briefly in front of Sam's bloodshot panic-filled eyes, and slowly began to encircle his head.

He was frozen too. With a languid slowness, the

tentacle wrapped itself about him, covering his ears, his nose, his eyes. When his face was completely covered, the brown snake squeezed, and Sam screamed. His hands flew up to claw at the sticky muck threatening to smother him. As it squeezed, it lost its snake-like form, flattened into a mask covering his whole head. It clung fast to Sam's skin. He sank to his knees, his hands scrabbling feebly. His screams, barely audible through the vomit mask, weakened and died. His body slumped facedown on the porch.

A moment passed. An owl hooted distantly. The dead eyes of extinguished jack-o'-lanterns stared at her vacantly from neighbors porches and stoops. Piles of leaves rustled nervously, snuggled against the curb. Sheet ghosts and cackling plastic witches hung from tree limbs spun lazily in the night breeze.

"Sam?" June's heart was racing, her hands shaking, her entire being laser-focused on the unmoving body of her friend. Adrenaline pulsed through her bloodstream. She inched forward, bent to roll him over.

Sam's head snapped up. Where the mask covered his face, the stinking brown sludge boiled and bubbled. It smelled sweet and burnt and horrible. Something moved beneath the roiling surface. Aghast, June jumped back, butt pressed against the door. A subtle rumbling sound reached her ears, something like a cafeteria full of open-mouthed chewers or a writhing mass of maggots. It was punctuated with snaps and pops like Rice Krispies in milk. Hollows formed in the mask. Two sunken eye sockets, vacant and black, suddenly filled with one gleaming peppermint candy each, white and red—

bloodshot. A gaping maw, yawning open like a haunted cave, slowly filling with candy corn teeth, yellow, orange, and white-tipped stalagmites and stalactites slowly emerging from the brown muck, razor-sharp. The mouth exhaled a noxious breath and stretched into a malevolent grin, and June screamed. She watched red licorice veins rise to the surface and pulse in its forehead. Tootsie Roll lips formed around its mouth, and a bubblegum tongue emerged and licked their perimeter. Thick caramel drool oozed out. The expression on the creature's face, the creature that once had been Sam, was pure hunger.

Something clicked in June's brain, some long-dormant, predator/prey, fight-or-flight instinct, and she flung the door open and bolted inside, slammed it behind her, and locked it tight. The candy creature immediately slammed against it and roared, a low bellow of rage and frustration.

"MOM! DAD!" June screamed, sprinting upstairs two steps at a time. She skidded to a stop outside her parents' room. Their bed was empty.

What the hell? Where were they?

She flew back downstairs, still screaming, the panic rising in her like a wave, threatening to drown all coherent thought. She ran through the living room: no sign of them. The kitchen empty.

She heard a thump from the dining room and beelined toward it, skidding to a stop in the doorway. Her father was kneeling beneath the table, his back to June. A chair was overturned.

"Dad?"

His head turned slowly toward her, revealing what she feared: a chocolate brown mask covered his face.

Gummy worm eyebrows wriggled with amusement above gumdrop eyes. The Dad-creature chewed, swallowed, and opened its mouth in a hideous grin. Crimson blood was smeared across its rock candy mustache and dripped from its stick-candy teeth, which were sharpened to cruel points.

June's mother was sprawled on her back beneath him. She was unconscious but breathing. A sizable chunk of flesh was gnawed away from her thigh. Blood pooled beneath her.

June was frozen again, motionless except for her eyes that flicked wildly around the room, desperately gathering data, seeking escape routes, weapons—absorbing everything except the tableau of horror immediately before her. A cardboard witch dangled from the light fixture. A pumpkin spice candle sat unlit. June's Halloween candy was spread across the table. Empty wrappers. An orange one with a pumpkin winked at her. Her insulin kit.

An idea sprouted and bloomed in June's frantic mind, covered her consciousness like a warm blanket. Her insulin kit. Sugar's worst enemy.

Something that was once Sam slammed against the front door again, somewhere behind her. A siren wailed in the distance.

The monster wearing her father's body lunged at June. At the same moment, she overturned the dining room table and lunged for the insulin, creating a barrier and spilling the candy she'd gathered for her parents all over the floor. The monster slipped in the mess of confectionary, stumbled, its bloody fingers groping for her—but June was fast, dodging away, snatching up the insulin kit. In deft movements, she uncapped the pen, screwed on a needle, and twisted the dose adjustment dial to 10 units. She'd never taken that much insulin herself. Ten units was enough to correct for a whole carton of ice cream.

Holding the loaded insulin pen like a dagger, June dashed to the kitchen. The monster was rising from the candy pile, but slowly, unsteadily gaining its feet. June grabbed a big cooking spoon from the utensil drawer, took the big bulk peanut butter jar down from the snack cabinet. She twisted it open and scooped out an enormous dollop. The sticky tan mass trembled on the spoon.

Silently praying her plan would work, June marched back toward the creature, peanut butter spoon in one hand, insulin pen in the other. It pinwheeled its arms for balance and leaned toward her, its spike-filled blood-dripping maw agape. With a flick of the wrist, June catapulted her spoon's contents into its mouth, which was immediately clogged with the thick peanut butter. The monster slipped to the floor, hands clawing to clear the gummy blockage.

June sprang forward again. With the creature incapacitated tooth and claw, she drove the insulin pen needle deep into the brown skin of its cheek and pressed the injection button. The payload of synthetic hormone pumped into the chocolate flesh. June retreated, staring intently at her adversary. It seemed oblivious to the dose she'd administered.

Moments passed. Nothing happened, and June's heart sank. She imagined the sweet teeth sinking into her skin. Would it feel like her insulin shots? Her lancet fingersticks? Certainly, much worse.

The chocolate-faced monster abruptly stopped clawing at the peanut butter in its mouth. It gazed at June with a look of confused horror, mouth twisted into a grimace. A muffled moan emanated from the creature. It shivered violently, and green smoke poured from its eyes and mouth. Taffy and caramel oozed from its pores, and its shiver graduated to full-on shake. Its body quaked like a dying leaf in the autumn wind. June was filled with ecstatic joy as she watched the chocolate mask melt from her father's face, dropping brown globs onto the dining room floor.

Within moments, her father was free. His face looked flushed but unblemished. He remained unconscious next to the steaming pile of sludge that had possessed him.

Monster-Sam crashed through the dining room window, snarling madly, bloodshot peppermint eyes aflame. Its candy corn teeth gnashed, and Tootsie Roll lips dripped caramel slobber. Broken glass tinkled. The enraged creature loomed between June and the kitchen, panting and grinning hungrily.

Cut off from her peanut butter, June spun on her heels and darted toward the living room, twisting her insulin pen's dose adjustment dial back to 10. Monster-Sam lurched after her.

June's foot slipped on the spilled candy. She lost her balance and could not regain it. As she fell, time slowed. As she watched the floor approach in slow motion, she noticed the wrapper underfoot was a Reese's. Betrayed, she thought bitterly. For a moment, she gazed at her unconscious parents, lying in their respective puddles of crimson and ochre fluid, and felt a pang of love and concern so strong she thought she might cry. Instead, she squeezed her eyes shut and prepared for impact.

June hit the ground and covered her head, insulin pen raised in blind defense. If the creature plowed into her, her needle would be the first thing it'd run into. She braced herself, thumb trembling over the injection button.

No impact came.

She looked up. The monster stood gazing toward the broken window. Its cocked head twitched every few moments. Its shard-filled mouth hung open, lips slack, dripping beads of caramel to the floor. It seemed mesmerized like it could hear some captivating melody June couldn't, and she thought again of a cobra in a woven pot enraptured by its snake charmer. Moving like a sleepwalker, monster-Sam walked calmly over the broken glass and climbed out the window.

June kneeled at her father's side and shook him gently. He was breathing but did not wake. Her mother she did not disturb, but carefully wrapped a kitchen towel around her leg wound. She dialed 911 and left the phone off the hook, hoping the operator could trace the call and send emergency services.

She had to follow Sam to cure him like she had her father.

She kissed both parents on the cheek, grabbed her jacket, and—still clutching her insulin pen—followed the candy-faced monster that had once been her best friend out the window into the crisp autumn night.

The faceless thing stood in the cemetery, its black cloak rippling in the breeze. Its black bowl of Choco-'-Lanterns, now mostly empty, sat on the ground behind it. The secret recipe had done its job. Children gathered among the headstones, between spiderwebbed mausoleums and weathered statues. What had once been children. Chocolate faces stared slack-jawed at the faceless thing. It was nearly the hour of the taking.

No adults had been called. Leached of youth and innocence by time's passage, their flesh did not slake the faceless thing's appetite. The sweet madness overtook all who underwent the change, but adults who succumbed were simply not summoned. After the ritual was complete, every mask left on this plane would consume the flesh of its wearer, digesting skull bone, grey matter. Identity erased. The natural way, *the faceless thing thought.* To eat and be eaten.

The hour of the taking had come. The faceless thing raised its hands over the masked congregation. Blood dripped from mouths once filled with baby teeth, now filled with rows of hard candy fangs, peppermint tusks, and jagged confectionery chompers. Gummy worm lips curled in dumb smiles.

The ritual began.

June crouched behind a tall gravestone at the edge of the cemetery. Years of weathering had worn it smooth, making its inscription unreadable. The Sam-creature stood a few yards beyond her, near a moss-covered angel statue missing its head. The creature swayed gently and occasionally twitched.

They both stared at the dark figure at the center of the cemetery. It wore a winking jack-o'-lantern mask, the same design from the Choc-o'-Lantern candy June had watched Sam eat.

With slow grace, the figure raised its hands, like a pastor giving a benediction. The children sighed in unison, the gentle seashell sound like a distant wave crashing on a midnight beach.

June glanced around at them. They were oblivious to her, all their attention focused on the dark figure.

Seemingly satisfied, the figure removed its orange mask, peeling it away like the plastic around a candy apple.

June barely stifled a scream. This figure was no man.

The thing's skin was wrinkled and pox-ridden, covered in pus-filled sores and patches of blue-green mold. The sores wept yellow rivulets of gore. It had no eyes, no mouth, no nose, no ears. A lone spider crawled lazily down the wrecked terrain of its face.

The figure languidly tossed aside its cloak, revealing a lean and twisted body, its limbs like pumpkin vines, jointed in too many places. Giant black bruises blotched its skin. Its long thin fingers moved like spider legs.

It beckoned to a child in the crowd.

Enraptured, the girl came forward. She was still dressed in her costume from the neck down, a striped tiger outfit with a dangling orange tail. Her face was a chocolate ruin. Wide jawbreaker eyes gazed at the beckoning creature. Slightly agape, her mouth displayed a row of Bananarama teeth, sharp as fish hooks.

The faceless thing proffered a twisted hand, and the girl took it. The creature raised its other hand with its index finger lifted. The slender finger elongated and sharpened until it became a vicious thorny claw. The faceless thing extended it down toward the girl's captured paw.

June's eyes were wide with disbelief and horror.

The claw tore into the girl's palm, spilling blood. The girl did not recoil but remained silent, calmly focused.

Where the blood fell, it pooled and began to smoke. The cemetery soil beneath roiled, as if liquefied, and a black pit opened—a chasm in the earth. Roots and bones protruded from the packed-earth walls. Ebony steps led down into deep subterranean blackness. A low-pitched otherworldly drone filled June's ears like the distant buzzing of a colossal hornet.

The girl with the bleeding hand stepped into the pit. She was immediately swallowed by darkness.

The faceless thing raised its hands again, its palms upturned this time, and made a come-hither motion to the entire crowd of masked children that stood silent in the cemetery. The children immediately shuffled forward toward the opening in the earth.

The ritual was nearly complete. The portal was opened. The faceless thing's harvest was prepared. It had only to shepherd the children into his crypt.

The faceless thing reflected upon the ceremony to come. Deep within the earth, it would drain each child of its precious innocent blood, the blood that kept the thing alive for centuries. The blood was stored in great black vats covered in arcane symbols only the faceless thing could read.

Next, the thing would harvest each child's store of rich creamy fat, which it would render into lard to use in next year's secret recipe.

The chocolate masks were an integral part of this process, keeping each exsanguinated child alive throughout it.

They transformed each child into a new faceless thing as its blood drained. Twisted, bloodthirsty perversions of humanity. Fresh seeds of evil thrown to the wind.

The faceless thing shepherded the first child into the void it called home.

June was terrified but knew she had to act fast. She couldn't lose Sam to that hole in the ground.

The kids were shuffling into a queue that led to the chasm.

A pair of rusted hedge clippers rested next to a

nearby headstone, left by some forgetful groundskeeper, June surmised. She tucked her insulin pen into her pajama pocket and picked up the clippers.

Crouching low, June crept around the perimeter of the cemetery, silent as a mouse, careful to keep a headstone or mausoleum between herself and the faceless thing at all times.

Within minutes, June was pressed against a headstone, mere yards behind the monster.

She took a deep breath and tightened her grip on the shears.

The children filed underground. The faceless thing swelled with triumph. This Halloween had brought the most bountiful harvest yet. His body shivered with delight, eager to bathe in their innocent blood.

Suddenly, the faceless thing felt cool iron blades bite into the skin of its thin right ankle. Pain screamed through its mind like hot lightning. It toppled to the ground, its right foot severed. The faceless thing writhed in the wet grass, clutching its stump. It raised its shriveled head in disbelief to behold the maskless child who stood over it, brandishing pruning shears. The faceless thing thrust its thorned finger toward the interloper, hoping to discourage further attack, but the shears clamped down upon its wrist and squeezed. Hand separated from arm and fell to the wet grass beside it.

The flow of children into the crypt had halted.

They gazed dumbly at the twisted figure writhing on the ground and the smaller figure standing above it.

Filled with fury, the faceless thing tried to rise, but the child kicked it back down and slashed at it with the clippers. The child kicked it again, rolling it toward the gaping hole in the earth.

Adrenaline pumped wildly through June's bloodstream. She kicked the creature again, driving it closer to the crypt entrance. She prayed this would work.

She kicked the faceless thing into the hole and heard it clatter and roll down the black steps.

She turned and picked up the creature's severed hand. She shivered. Its flesh was cold and stiff.

Carefully, she used the sharp tip of its index finger to pierce her own fingertip before dropping the hand into the hole.

Dull scraping sounds echoed up the passageway as the faceless thing struggled to drag itself back up the steps.

She squeezed her pricked finger, and a drop of blood welled up. It fell to the ground, a single crimson teardrop.

Blood opened the chasm. Maybe blood would close it.

As June's blood soaked into the earth, the drone intensified in volume until it grew to a dull roar. The walls of the passageway started to collapse.

The scrabbling sounds intensified and became frantic.

A gust of wind blew through the cemetery, a whirlwind of crimson leaves dancing among the granite markers. An animal screamed.

Before the hole closed completely, June tossed in the severed foot.

The shadow of the monster had almost reached the top step when the earth collapsed, sealing tight like a healed wound. The grass didn't even look disturbed, as if the hole never existed at all.

The monster was gone.

All around her, the children's masks were melting. Chocolate dribbled to the ground, revealing smooth rosy faces. Brown piles flecked with candy pieces littered the cemetery like cow-pies. Kids slumped unconscious between headstones.

June spotted Sam and ran to him. She kneeled beside him in the wet grass. His face was clean, and he wore a peaceful expression. He was unconscious but okay. He wasn't a monster anymore.

Police sirens warbled in the distance. June rose and realized her hands were shaking, and her heart was pounding like a snare drum.

Was her sugar low?

It had been around 3:30 AM when she tested after her nightmare. That nightmare seemed like kid stuff compared to this one—the waking one she'd just experienced.

She had walked all the way from her house to the cemetery. And her fight with the faceless thing had been pretty intense. Her sugar had likely dropped from all that physical exertion.

Her testing supplies were still in her bedroom, blocks away. No way to know how bad it was.

June felt panic rising in her throat. She couldn't make it home like this. She'd have a seizure, die shaking like a leaf on the sidewalk.

There was a bowl of candy on the ground. Winking jack-o'-lanterns printed on orange wrappers, deviously grinning up at her. Choc-o'-Lanterns.

Did these really turn Dad and Sam into monsters?

Surely the dark magic was gone now. Melted away like the chocolate masks. Scattered on the autumn wind like so many fallen leaves.

June unwrapped the candy and held it in her trembling palm.

Before it could melt, she ate it.

➤➤ **RECIPE** ◀◀
Choc-O'-Lanterns

1/2 cup heavy cream
6 oz. (1 cup) chopped bittersweet chocolate
1/2 tsp. vanilla
2 lbs. tempered semi-sweet chocolate
Jack-o'-Lantern candy molds

Place the chopped bittersweet chocolate in a medium bowl, and set aside. Pour the heavy cream into a small saucepan over medium heat, bring it to a simmer.

Once the cream is near boiling, pour the hot cream over the chopped chocolate and let it sit for one minute to soften the chocolate.

Gently whisk the cream and chocolate together until smooth and homogeneous. Add vanilla extract and stir to blend. Press a piece of cling wrap to the top of the ganache and let it sit at room temperature to cool.

While you wait for the ganache to cool, prepare the molds. If you have only one mold, you will have to repeat this process multiple times until all of your candies are formed. If you have multiple molds, you can do this all in one batch. Take the tempered chocolate, and spoon some into each cavity in the mold, so that the cavities are entirely filled.

Wait about a minute, then flip the mold upside down over a piece of parchment paper. The excess chocolate will drip down onto the paper. Swirl it slightly to encourage the chocolate to drip down.

Take a chef's knife, an offset spatula, or a bench scraper, and run it across the top of the mold, removing any excess chocolate from the top.

Let the chocolate mold harden at room temperature, or if your ganache is ready (completely cool but still runny) to use immediately, place the mold in the refrigerator to quickly set it for about 10 minutes.

Once set, spoon or pipe the ganache into your molds, filling each cavity 3/4 full. Tap the molds on the counter to release any air bubbles. Refrigerate the molds to firm up the ganache, for about 30 to 45 minutes. It needs to be firm enough so that when you put warm melted chocolate on top of it, it will hold its shape and not melt into the chocolate.

This is the ideal place within the process to insert your own customized curse or spellwork into the chocolate.

Once the ganache is chilled and firm, re-temper the chocolate and spoon some melted chocolate on top of each cavity, spreading it to the edges so the ganache is completely sealed in.

Scrape off the excess again with your knife or bench scraper, until the chocolate layer is completely flat with the top of the mold.

Allow the chocolates to completely set at room temperature or in the refrigerator, then turn the mold upside-down and gently tap them out of the mold. If necessary.

Wrap tightly in orange Cellophane.

Serve.

Threading the Needle

Kristi Petersen Schoonover

eath came to Nana's village when she made sauerbraten.

"I was the *nositel*. The Bringer." Nana's thick, liver-spotted hands looped the crochet hooks, which the convalescent home only allowed if they weren't sharp. I knew it made the yarn more difficult to work—as her only granddaughter, she'd taught me when I was seven. It'd been at least thirty years, though, since I'd even considered picking it up again. "I didn't want to do it, but it was the way of things there."

"A bringer of what?" I asked.

"A peaceful end."

I'd grown up in Nana's house, and she'd lived with my husband Everett and me until she'd fallen ill a few weeks ago. I'd never heard her mention this. Then again, she'd never shared much about her early life in a Central European village I can't pronounce. Sometime over the past ninety years, the place had been forgotten by mapmakers—possibly even by everyone *but* Nana—and this sounded like one of its buried folktales even if I *did* feel a chill frost my heart.

The Bringer ended the lives of the tortured, the sick, the broken-hearted. Always a desperate knock roused her from sleep, and a defeated loved one stood hunched beneath the weight of a freshly slain animal. No words were spoken. Nana took the offering, threaded it with poisoned strips of lard, and made the meal. It was, *usually* willingly, eaten by the afflicted.

Within a day, the village was gathered at the cemetery.

"I was angry when it was done to my *matka*, that the Bringer could let me, such a small girl, go without her mother." She finished her crochet cord with a quick, neat pull. "But one night, the larding needle landed under my pillow. And I understood it is a thing you can*not* refuse to do."

I didn't know what a larding needle was, so I Googled it on my phone. I didn't like what I saw. It looked like a slightly bent lance with a sharp tip, the length of someone's forearm, and had a clip on the opposite end full of alligator-like teeth.

As if that weren't disturbing enough, the previous Bringer's last name was Kučeřík, and he, apparently, had denied the privilege to his wife. After the death of her unborn child, she'd fled many times to the river and tried to drown herself. Her husband always intervened. "Poor Mrs. Kučeříková. For three years, she wandered, eyes empty. She didn't bathe or market," Nana said. "She would weep in the night. Everyone heard it. Finally, she managed to do it. She was floating in the river."

The needle came to my Nana that February, the

coldest one the mountains had seen in recent memory. Her father made her bring milk to Kučeřík. She arrived to find him standing, knee-deep in snow, atop his barn roof. He poked out his eyes with the larding needle and then shot himself.

"It's selfish to make someone suffer just because you want them to stay. Hand me my carry." She reached her hand out for the basket where she kept her crochet accoutrements; it was on the floor at the foot of her bed.

I grabbed its worn handle and passed it to her.

Her hands were ice. "Someone must do it for me. I don't have long."

"We'll have none of that talk now!" It was Peg, one of Nana's nurses. She always wore her silver hair in a bob and smelled like sugar cookies. She had taken a strong liking to Nana and to me.

"She's just telling me stories from the Old World," I said. "Right, Nana?"

Peg looked at me. "Visiting hours are just about done for today, Betta, just a reminder." She straightened the pillows on Nana's bed. "I'll be back."

After Peg had gone, Nana shifted the just-fixed bedding. "There was an accident, a fire, far away to *us* then, but now I know how close it was. Mostly everyone in the village got sick. So many came to the door, begging for me to put their mother or sister or brother or husband out of misery. My first mercy was a little girl. I can't remember her name now. She'd been swimming in the river. Her skin was like paper, and she was black and red. I saw her innards through her skin."

A week later, those left were evacuated. She ended

up here in America, a girl of fifteen with nothing but a single suitcase containing her beloved matroschka dolls, a photo of her *matka*, and a few dresses.

"Once the first life is taken, the needle must pass on. Someday, it will come to you." She closed her eyes. "And I will expect you to relieve me of my suffering."

That was enough. I was actually terrified. "Nana—"

"It is a thing you cannot refuse to do."

"Of course," I said.

It was a story. That was all.

Right?

Besides, I'd seen her debone chickens, chop purple cabbage, and fling *nokedli* into boiling water. I'd eaten her fricassee, cucumber salad, and lamb stew.

Surely, there was a nonlethal version of sauerbraten.

Why had I never seen her thread *anything* through any kind of meat? *Why had I never eaten this dish?*

Everett and I had been doing the cooking since she'd gone to the facility, so if there had been a larding needle anywhere in that kitchen, we would've found it. After all, nothing had changed in the way we ate dinner together—except, of course, for the fact that we didn't have to set an extra plate, because now there were two of us, not three. Nana insisted that an odd number of plates at the table brought bad luck.

On the ride home to Tiverton, I rolled down my window, reveling in the scent of the ocean as I crossed over the Mount Hope Bridge.

Outside the hospital walls, the tale seemed downright outlandish.

When I arrived at our white Colonial, Everett's Cross Country was in the driveway. It was only five-thirty; he shouldn't have been home from work yet. He worked in Boston, so it was at least an hour and a half commute each way. If there were an emergency—he was in medical IT; people's lives depended on equipment running properly—he'd often come home and find me passed out with an issue of *The Fiction Desk* across my chest.

"Baby?" The house smelled like my black currant candles and felt light and clean. The hardwood floors looked as though they'd been polished, and the white kitchen counters, which I could see from the foyer, were clutter-free. A bottle of wine and two glasses sat on the butcher block island.

Everett was many wonderful things, but romantic wasn't one of them. Not like this, anyway.

"Hello? Ev?"

He appeared in the archway, wearing gray sweatpants and an olive hoodie that had become his favorite since I'd bought it for him last Christmas. "Hey."

"What are you doing here? The place feels nice."

"Yeah, I forgot to tell you. I worked a half-day today."

I eyed him. He'd been a little down recently, and when I'd asked him about it, he'd said it was pressure at work. "Any reason why?"

"Nothing like *that*, no." He shrugged. "Couple of errands to run. *And* I fixed the upstairs toilet."

There really hadn't been much choice there—the seal at the bottom of the tank was disintegrating, so there had been a leak for a week or so. To leave it unrepaired was to risk ruining the dining room ceiling. I set my bags down on the mail table. "And that's worth candles and wine?"

"Sure. You won't have to nag. Come." He held out his meaty hand—one of the things that always attracted me to him. His hands were, literally, twice the size of mine. "Let's sit outside."

I'd gone to see Nana directly from my office. "Just let me get into my comfies."

He nodded. "Okay."

On my way out, I stopped. Nana's wing of the house was off the kitchen, at the end of a long hall. I hesitated for a moment. She hadn't been there in weeks, and even though I'd gone in a few times to drop off clean laundry, I respected her privacy, so I really didn't have much of an idea what was beyond that door. *Maybe the larding needle is in there.*

"It's gorgeous out here, babe!" Everett called from the back deck.

"Coming!" I hurried upstairs to our bedroom, changed quickly into the chemise set he'd bought me two birthdays ago. He was a tactile man and loved the feel of things, and I knew that this one, which was velvet, was his favorite.

This time, when I went past Nana's section of the house, I deliberately didn't look.

Our back deck jutted over a cliff and featured a stunning view of the bay and the Mount Hope Bridge.

I curled up against Everett on the wicker couch, comforted by his light smell of clove and pine. It was the end of September, but there were still plenty of boats tottering around like the last drunks at the party. The sky was a watercolor of orange and purple behind the silhouette of the bridge. A damp breeze stung my thinly clad form. He hummed in contentment as I huddled closer for warmth and set my head against his chest.

I knew instantly something wasn't right. I lifted my head and looked up at him. "What's wrong?"

"Nothing, why?"

"Your heart's racing."

"Oh, you know me. Home all day near the coffee pot. Too much caffeine." He tightened his arm around me. "How was your visit with Tess?" That was my Nana's nickname. Her real name was Terezie.

"Fine." I honestly didn't feel like rehashing.

The silence was broken only by the cries of a couple of mourning doves. On the bridge, the lights on the main cables popped on. It looked like three necklaces against the night sky.

"What, no stories? No 'I really love the crochet turtle she's making for kids we're never going to have, and that makes me sad?'"

"Stop." I hit him on the stomach.

"It's just not like you, is all."

"It was . . . well, the visit was kind of weird."

He rubbed my fingers with his thumb. "How so?"

There was nothing we hadn't shared with each other, not since the night we met. Back in college one night, I'd been trying to maneuver my car out of the mud hole that Three's Bar called a parking lot, and I plowed into his ancient Volvo. I could hear him yelling, but when I got out of the car, he just stood there and looked at me. We went to a nearby diner and had fries with malt vinegar, and that was the end of that.

Strangely, I thought better of telling him any specifics. "She told me about life in her village. Before she came here."

"And?"

"Just—"

"She scare you with a bunch of creepy folk tales again?"

I mused at how well he knew me. I supposed this story wasn't any worse than some of the others she'd told me when I was a kid, about soul-stealing Waternicks and castles with paper floors. "I guess she did."

"It's okay." He kissed my head, shifted me to sit forward, and grabbed the bottle of Nobilo. "This is a nice one. Not super-expensive, but you like New Zealands."

If you asked someone to choose his favorite time of day, he might say morning, when everything was quiet and promising, or afternoon, when the sun was a jewel in a clear sky, or sunset, when it was time to celebrate a job well done.

My favorite time of day was night, when it was all over; that was when I got to slip into bed next to him. The world was outside, there was nothing to intrude or hurt us, and nothing that'd happened that day mattered.

"Cheers." He passed me the glass.

I settled back against him, but even though I was in his arms, I couldn't get the image of a young Nana out of my mind. I saw her standing there with her suitcase, her matroschka doll and a photo of her *matka*, which she still had . . . and perhaps something else: that larding needle, the one that had belonged to the Bringer before her, and the Bringer before that, and the Bringer before that.

The one that Kučeřík had used to stab out his eyes.

I didn't sleep well. I'd drifted off in Everett's lap, and he'd roused my shivering body and guided me into bed, where he gathered me against him. But instead of feeling cocooned and safe, I was terrified by an assault of images: The larding needle. A haggard man with red eyes standing in the doorway. A dead buck, a slaughtered cow. My Nana, humming her favorite lullaby, "Hajej, Můj Andíliku." A matroschka doll. Everett's side of the bed, empty. Every time I awakened, there were shadows on the ceiling—the same innocuous ones I always saw when I got up and padded to our master bathroom, but on this night, they looked like greedy hands.

You are going to get that larding needle and get rid of it. As long as you think it's in this house, you're not going to get any rest.

I thought about taking care of it at that moment, but Everett would wonder why I was rummaging in Nana's room, and it was too much to explain. So I closed my eyes and waited it out.

In the morning, Everett—fully dressed in a suit and tie—kissed me on the cheek. "Hey, you going to work today? You're late."

"No." I was calling in. I was too exhausted to even think about sitting in front of a computer screen; I'd probably just nod off. "I have some appointments."

"Okay." He kissed me on the cheek. "I'll see you tonight."

"Mmmm." I stretched, stared out the picture window that looked out over the roofs of the houses that were below us on the cliff facing the bay. It was barely officially autumn, but the light had a sharp, winter look to it.

As soon as Everett had gone, I shrugged into his olive hoodie, which had landed at the foot of our bed. I went into the kitchen, poured myself a cup of coffee—hit with guilt that Everett had brewed it; that was always my job—and stood at the end of the hall, staring at Nana's door.

Just do it. You know it isn't in the kitchen, so if it's here, it's in with her things.

Half of me felt dirty, rooting through my beloved Nana's private country. But I reminded myself I was only looking; it wasn't as though I was sorting for an estate sale.

I shuddered at the thought.

I took one more slug of coffee and steeled myself.

The stale scent of Nana's lily of the valley perfume was oppressive, and for a moment, I thought of calling the whole thing off. Her monk's bench was crowded with crochet projects: teddy bears, snowmen, afghans. Her full-sized bed was still only half-made; she'd just started her morning routine when she'd collapsed, and we'd had to take her to the hospital. A framed rendering of Jesus and the photo of her mother sat on her dresser next to some empty walnut shells and one of my candles.

I went over to Jesus and turned him so he was facing the wall.

In her nightstands, I found only Bibles, pills, and blank notecards. Her closet held what you'd expect: her Lane Bryant dresses and extra-wide stack heels, her fancy hats that probably hadn't seen the sun since the Kennedy era, and, in a plastic tub at the bottom, several matching handbags that looked as though they'd only been used once.

No larding needle.

Next to the closet was a large bookcase. To anyone else, it might have seemed silly, but I was going to search this room clockwise to ensure I wasn't going to miss a thing. I went through every shelf with no result. I checked under the bed, behind the furniture. I opened each of her drawers. Bras, nightgowns, panty hose.

The bottom drawer was crammed with papers. Clippings from the sinking of the *Andrea Doria*, the moon landing, Watergate. What looked to be insurance policies, an old JC Penney catalogue, and instruction manuals for appliances that no longer existed. Tucked against the back of the drawer was her beautiful red matroschka doll, the one I remembered was always in the living room on the mantle. It had a large crack down its cherubic face and was partially split open. I should have seen the color of the second doll underneath, but it was blocked by something yellowed, like a slip of paper.

I picked up the doll, and it broke open in my hands. A large, jagged piece fell to the floor.

Shit.

The paper I'd seen had fallen out; I picked it up and turned it over. It was a photo of Nana, although she looked to be in her twenties, maybe, and she was in a wedding gown. She was standing next to a blonde man I didn't recognize. He was very handsome, with a chiseled jaw; it certainly wasn't Grampa Jay.

Had Nana had a husband *before him?*

How could I ask her about it without her knowing I was rooting around in her things?

I tried to set the photo and split matroschka pieces back in the drawer as best I could.

The en-suite bathroom was the last place to check. Several jars of stale-smelling powder, bottles of Cepacol, and stacks of hand towels later, I was convinced there was no larding needle and was about to move on when something else caught my attention.

On the shelf above the commode was a beat-up cigar box. Not large enough to hold a larding needle, but provocative just the same.

I opened it.

Mass cards, programs from funerals, and three small glass vials, each the height and thickness of my thumb. One had a clear liquid; the second, a brown powder; the third, some kind of black gelatin. Long expired perfumes and make-up, probably. I pushed them aside to reveal a pile of folded notes beneath—one, in particular, I'd made for her. *Oh, my God. She kept this?* I held it for a second, the memory of the day I'd made it so vivid. I wanted to open it, but thought twice. Honestly, I was haunted by everything I'd seen. I wanted out of her space.

Just take it with you. She isn't here. She isn't even going to know it's missing.

I'd checked every possible place in her suite. There was no larding needle.

It really *had* been just a story.

Satisfied, I left the room and closed the door behind me.

I would love you the second time, too!

I'd made her the note when I was seven. Both of my parents had skipped out, and so I lived with her and my Grampa Jay in a mansion on Ocean Drive in Newport.

I had my own wing, with a bay window in my bedroom that overlooked the ocean. While it was a peaceful sight and on summer nights a pleasure to push open the side panes and hear the wind, sometimes, my imagination would play tricks on me. The shimmering moon on the surface of the sea would transform into ghosts from the shipwrecks I read about, or I'd think I'd see my parents and hear them calling my name. I never knew where they'd gone, and if I asked, Nana would just tell me they were someplace that wasn't safe for me, and that's why I was better off with her. When I was an adult, I'd asked her about them again, and she told me she actually had no idea what had happened to them.

It was early in the morning, and I was at the mahogany table in the dining room. A thunderstorm shook the house, and rain lashed the windows. The day before, we'd been shopping downtown, and Nana had bought me a new set of colored pencils and a sketchbook since I'd declared I was going to be an artist someday. I remember I was only up at that time because I was so excited I couldn't wait to get started.

I tried to draw the potted palm tree in the corner.

Nana sat with her pills, her orange juice, and her toast, watching me. Grampa Jay, who, admittedly, wasn't a nice man, had no interest and was in the next room, where he atrophied in his chair next to a crystal dish full of Brach's butterscotch candies, watching the television on full volume. Every once in a while, the TV went silent—he normally muted the commercials, then groused to himself or called for Nana. "Mommy!"

"What do you want?" Nana crabbed. "I fed you already!"

"The TV's out!"

"It's because of the storm, you old man! So read your *Guideposts*. I'm sitting with my girl Betta." Nana worried a paper towel with her thick fingers. She thumbed and folded, creased and smoothed, then started over again. "The first time you marry for love, the second time you marry for money." She gestured to the other room. "Do you think I love *that*? Love is for the birds."

I didn't *really* understand, but I nodded because clearly, this was important wisdom that needed to be imparted. But I remember being horrified by the idea that you had to spend time with someone you didn't love. After all, my parents didn't love me, and they'd just left, and I'm sure we were all happier, right? I tore a page out of my new sketchbook and made Nana the note in purple pencil: *I would love you the second time, too!*

"That's nice, there," she'd said, and patted my hand. "You're a good girl. You are going to be just fine in this world."

I would love you the second time, too!

All these years later, I understood. My thoughts meandered to the mysterious groom in the picture I'd found. I was still on my first marriage and didn't, honestly, ever plan on a second.

I had married for love, and it was the opposite of "for the birds."

At my office, I stared at my computer, trying to answer the last few questions for a grant I was writing. Every time I started typing, all that came to my mind was Nana's groom. Who was he? What had happened to him? Was this the man she'd married for love? If so, her marriage to Grampa Jay—my dad's father—was even more tragic.

It was clear I wasn't going to be able to answer anyone else's questions until I could answer my own. At three o'clock, I gave up and drove to the facility.

"She's sleeping right now," Peg said when I arrived. "We'd prefer you just leave her be."

"I can wait."

Peg shrugged. "If you want, sure. Let me know if you need anything."

I sat for a good hour, just watching Nana breathe. She looked different . . . pale, drawn, and . . . *still*. I had never seen her sleep before, not even when I was a kid. Somehow, I'd always thought that she *didn't* sleep. That giant mansion was always dust-free. There were always fresh lekvár-stuffed crepes at breakfast, pound cakes after school, hearty slow-cooks for dinner. There were always new crocheted animals and two Christmas trees, and I'm pretty sure she never forgot anyone's birthday—she was always taking cards or boxes to the post office. "I'll sleep when I'm dead," she always said.

I tried to keep my mind from going to the place where I'd be looking at her in her coffin, but I couldn't.

What I was looking at now was probably what she was going to look like.

Someone must do it for me. I don't have long.

The thought made me anxious. And sick. And scared.

On my way out, Peg looked up from her clipboard. "Oh, I meant to ask you, Betta—just as she was drifting off to sleep, she said something about you might be bringing her something?"

I was startled. "What?"

"You were bringing her something. She didn't say what."

My blood ran cold because I knew what that really meant.

"Betta?"

I didn't respond.

"Hello? Are you okay?" Peg asked.

"Oh—sorry. What did you say?"

"I said, 'Did you bring something you wanted me to give her?'"

"Um—no. I—she asked for some new yarn, and I forgot it."

Peg smiled sweetly. "Okay. Shall I tell her you were here?"

"I'll—I'll be back tomorrow." Right then, I wanted to just be gone. Be out of this place that smelled clinical and lonely.

I couldn't get to my car fast enough, couldn't drive fast enough. Couldn't outrun the realization that Nana hadn't looked good. That she was going downhill. That the end was coming. That even worse, she believed I was going to be the *means* to that end. I told myself repeatedly, chanted it like a mantra, *it's just a story, it's just a story*, but it was little balm.

Everett's car was in the driveway. I walked into the house, threw my keys on the mail table, and called for him, but he didn't answer. He wasn't on the back deck. I went upstairs.

I heard the shower running.

I didn't knock. I went into the bathroom, slammed the door behind me, pressed my back against it.

"Babe, that you?" he asked.

I could barely speak. "Yeah."

"Gimmie a sec. Just washing the day off me." He turned off the water, slid open the shower curtain. The metal hooks jangled on the rod. He reached for the towel, started wiping himself down. "Listen, can we talk?"

"Nana's not doing well." I burst into tears.

I heard him heave a deep sigh. "Okay." He stepped out of the shower and pressed me against him. His skin was wet and warm and smelled like Dove body wash.

I cried for a long time.

Several minutes after I'd calmed, he said, "Bet I can take your mind off it."

I could feel my cheeks flush, a sudden need coursing its way through me, and I nodded, and the towel fell to the floor as he started right there with his hands under my dress. He pushed off my suit jacket, slipped the spaghetti straps from my shoulders, whispered for me to get out of my bra.

He tasted like wine.

We groped our way to the bed, and he pushed me down across it. I'd come to love his paunch as we'd aged, and suddenly it didn't feel right. Smaller, somehow, and when he pressed on top of me, I felt what I'd swear was his hipbone. "Ev."

He was busy with my neck. "What, baby?"

"Can we—can we move? Awkward position."

He didn't even come up for air, just manipulated the word against my collarbone. "Sure."

We shifted, and when my head hit the pillow, it struck something hard. My breath caught in my throat.

He stopped. "Talk to me."

"No, I'm good." I looked into his worried eyes. "Keep going."

He kissed behind my ears and on my neck.

I tried to focus on him, the feel of his back beneath my hands, the sculpt of his arm muscles, the down of his chest hair. The erasure of every thought, the electric pulse when he touched me, the shortness of my breath.

But *God*, whatever it was sat squarely at the base of my skull. I lifted my head and slid my hands beneath my pillow. The tips of my fingers came up against something cold and sharp.

What the hell is that?

But I knew damn well, deep inside, what it was.

He entered me, hard, and the force of it made my hands shove the object toward the wall-mounted headboard. It clattered to the floor beneath the bed.

Shit.

He stopped. "What was *that*?"

"Nothing," I gasped. "Stuff from the nightstand."

This time he didn't let it faze him. He went faster and finished, but for the first time in our lives, I had to fake it.

The next morning, while Everett was in the shower, I got up and peered under the bed to look at the thing. Half of me prayed it wasn't what I thought it was, but half of me prayed that it was so that I could banish it from the house and be done with this once and for all.

It was resting just beyond my reach; I was going to have to pull the bed out. When I did, it made a loud scraping groan, loud enough that Everett might have heard it over the sprinkling of our rainforest showerhead. I cringed.

I still heard the water running. Nothing changed.

I heaved a sigh of relief.

I lay down on the bed to pluck it from above. When I grabbed it, I got stung—*shit,* I'd cut myself on the tip. I watched as blood dripped onto the hardwood below and stuck my index finger in my mouth to keep it from getting all over the sheets.

Finally, I fished it up next to me.

It was a larding needle.

It didn't look like the thing I'd seen on Google. It was still lance-like, but thinner—like a knitting needle—and the tip, which was what I'd stabbed my finger on, was sharp as hell. Instead of the alligator clip at the one end, there was a ring at the end of a wooden handle, worn and dirty from age and use. The steel, though, was clean—not a speck of rust or dirt.

I felt like I was going to throw up or run screaming or both. It had been nowhere in the house. *How the hell had it gotten under my pillow?*

I heard Everett turn off the shower. Still nursing my injured finger, I pushed the needle back under the bed and hurried downstairs. I always had his coffee ready for him; he might know something was up if I didn't. I wrapped my finger in a Band-aid, but slipped into autopilot after that, just staring at the coffee while it brewed.

Everett embraced me from behind. "That was fantastic last night." He nuzzled into my neck. His familiar smell of clove and pine made me want him again—and it wouldn't be unheard of for us to make love in the a.m., which usually made him late for work—but I batted the thought away. I had a much more urgent concern.

He pulled away. "I've *still* got it."

It seemed like an odd thing for him to say; he was aware all he had to do was look at me. But I was relieved he'd apparently forgotten about the clatter of the scary instrument, so I just agreed. "You *do*."

"Alright. I'm out."

His travel mug was next to the brewer. He hadn't filled it. "Don't forget your coffee."

He looked pale. "Nah. Stomach's a bit off today."

He'd always had an iron system. "If you hang out for a minute, I can make you a tea."

"No, honey. It's fine. Probably just a bug. Better off with nothing." He slung his messenger bag over his shoulder and left.

The house was quiet.

I went upstairs and pulled out the larding needle. I sat with it on my lap, trying not to flee in terror. Then I recalled something more frightening: Nana said that when it came to me, I would have to end her suffering.

No.

A thousand times, *no*.

March this out to the trash right now.

My fingers throbbed, my heart raced, I felt like I couldn't breathe.

Now.

I raced downstairs to the garage, wrapped the needle in two extra-thick leaf collection bags, and tossed it in the large can. But when I started to walk away, I felt dizzy. My legs buckled. My body went numb with that pins-and-needles feeling that attacks a limb when you've been sitting on it too long, and the circulation's been cut off.

I collapsed to the concrete floor. It was cold.

Blackness nibbled at the edges of my consciousness.

"No!" I tried to form the word, but couldn't quite do it.

What the hell was going on?

My legs were dead weight. I crawled toward the large can—there was a metal bar on the wall next to it, where Everett hung cleaning rags. It was like a shower bar; I could use it to try to haul myself up.

I set my hand on the trash can and reached for the bar.

All the feeling came back, and I could breathe.

I grabbed the bar with both hands, started to pull.

The pins and needles returned.

Wait a minute.

I set my hand on the can.

I felt fine.

Jesus.

It wasn't going to let me get rid of it.

I kept my hands on the can, stood up, and took the wrapped needle out of the bag.

I brought it back in the house and shoved it in the drawer with my chemises.

Shaken, I called work and told them I'd be in later this afternoon. Then I took a quick shower and drove to the facility.

"She's been asking for you," Peg said as I rushed by, and when I didn't respond, she leaned over her desk and shouted, "She asked again about bringing her something!"

I entered Nana's room. They'd positioned her bed so that she was only half sitting up, and she looked even worse than when she'd been asleep—she was smaller, somehow. This very large woman whose favorite thing to do was eat a whole gallon of Breyers mint chocolate chip ice cream while she watched reruns of *Columbo* looked nearly emaciated and disinterested, and how had she lost that much weight in only a few days? Yes, she'd been getting thinner since she'd been here, but not like this.

Her crochet hooks and yarn were in the carry where I'd left them two days before.

She was humming her favorite lullaby, the one that I knew in English was called "My Little Angel." She stopped mid-note when she saw me.

I stood, out of breath, in her doorway. "Do you remember when you told me about marrying a second time for money?"

She turned her face toward me. She wore one of her favorite blouses, the one that had the embroidered apples. It was slightly yellowed and sported a chocolate-colored stain just below the neckline. "Why?"

"Were you—" I stopped. Why was I so afraid to ask this? I knew what the answer was; it was in the photo. I just didn't want to know what the follow-up answers were. "Were you married before?"

She moved her lips but said nothing, looked down and smoothed the blanket across her lap.

"Nana, what happened? Did he *die?*"

She sighed. "It was very sad, dear. He got sick; it was no good. I had to be a good Bringer."

It was a gut-punch. *Holy shit.*

"You—"

"I gave him his supper. That was all." A placid smile came over her face. "It came to you."

I hadn't planned on telling her, because I knew if I did she'd ask me to do the unthinkable. But I could never really lie to my Nana. "It did."

She nodded. "I knew it would. There is no one left in my village."

I felt pressure on my chest. "Then there is no one from your village who remembers this. I will never have to do it."

She eyed me, and it felt like she was looking right *through* me. "You must do it for me."

"No."

"Don't worry. It gets easier after the first time."

"There won't be a first time."

Her gaze became hard. She was *angry*. "True love is never selfish. Sometimes it means ending a person's suffering no matter how much you will miss her."

I didn't want her to be angry with me. Maybe I could reason with her logically. I stepped into the room and pulled the cushioned chair alongside her bed, sat down. "I don't even know how to make sauerbraten, and where would I get my hands on any poison?"

"You will know all the things when it's time."

"If they found the poison in your system, I would get arrested and go to jail."

"They won't." She patted my hand. "It is the way things are meant to be."

"I don't want to do this, Nana."

"You have to."

I stood up. "I'm not doing this."

"You need to be my good Betta."

"I can't."

"You cannot refuse," she said.

I was frustrated. Desperate to hear a different answer. *"Why?"*

"I don't want to talk about this anymore." She turned away from me and stared out the window. There was a rumble of thunder, and it started to rain.

I hadn't gotten far from the facility when I was consumed by a compulsion to stop at Clements' Marketplace. It was urgent and maddening, like needing to pee: all I could think about, and going to happen whether it was convenient or not.

Even if I damn well knew we didn't need groceries. We'd done the shopping on Saturday and were stocked.

I'd been a customer of Clements' since I was a kid. It was the Portsmouth IGA then, and Nana traveled the half-hour from Newport just because it had a great butcher counter.

The butcher counter, I thought. *The butcher counter is the most important thing.*

My God, what was happening to me?

I parked, pulled several recyclable bags from my back seat, and made my way into the store with a list of items in my head: cheesecloth, dried ginger root, whole mace (what *was* that, anyway?). Lard, celery and parsley roots, bacon. Some were things I'd never bought in my life, and yet, somehow, I knew where they were. It was almost as though the cart made a beeline, blowing past my staples: Kalamata olives and herbed goat cheese, chicken breast, and rosemary crackers.

I knew exactly what was going on.

I was getting the ingredients I needed to make Nana's sauerbraten.

I tried to let go of the cart. I tried to walk away. I

couldn't. I grabbed a large onion like it was a coveted jewel, selected the cinnamon sticks and carrots as though lives depended upon their condition.

People stared.

I found myself at the butcher counter. A smiling older man with a ruddy face asked in a phlegmy voice if he could help.

The only word I had in my head was *meat*.

What should I choose? Lamb or venison? Bison or beef? There were marbled slabs and bloody boulders, briskets and tenderloins, and roasts.

It was the last thing in the case that called to me: a whole boneless sirloin, which dwarfed every chunk of flesh near it. It sat, unwrapped, on a metal tray, in a pool of blood, its layer of fat a sickly yellowish pink and veiny. "I'll have that one." I pointed to the behemoth.

Ruddy Face nodded cheerfully, but instead of opening the glass case and reaching inside, he turned and went through the large brown swinging doors on the back wall. In a few minutes, he reappeared with a newly wrapped, but different, boneless sirloin.

I was furious. "I asked for that one."

He tried to maintain an upbeat demeanor, but I could see he was annoyed. He cleared his throat. "It's the same thing."

I glared at him.

"Don't you trust me?"

"No." I pointed to the original hunk I'd selected. "I want *that* piece of meat. Specifically. *That one.*"

He grimaced and leaned over the counter. The giant smear of meat blood on his apron made it look as though he'd just killed someone. "That one's not as fresh—really, we just use it for display."

"I don't care. That's the one I want."

We locked expressions, but then he acquiesced. He opened the case, pulled out the tray, and took it to the counter, where he wrapped it, weighed it, and slapped on a white and purple sticker reading 16.92 lb/$84.43. "Good luck."

I don't know why, but I found the way he'd said it unsettling.

In the checkout line, I looked at the absurd line-up of items on the conveyor belt; none of them seemed to make sense. I just knew I needed them.

I *had* to have them.

When I got home, the first thing on my mind was that everything I bought was going in the trash. The mustard seed and black peppercorn, the cloves and vinegar, the just-baked white bread, the anointed sirloin.

In the trash, because I was *not* making sauerbraten.

I was not going to be the Bringer. I didn't know how I was going to change it, but I was. Somehow, I'd figure it out.

Seeing Everett's car in the driveway made all thoughts pass; he was home early, again. I lugged the recyclable bags into the house and hefted them onto the counter.

I saw him through the kitchen window. He was standing out by the deck railing, his back to me, looking out at the bay. There was a half-consumed bottle of wine and two glasses on the coffee table.

The groceries could wait. I stepped outside. "How was your day?"

He turned. He had his hands in his pockets. He looked overwhelmingly sad.

I took a step forward. "What is it?"

"I can't wait anymore. There's no easy way to say this."

There was the cry of a mourning dove.

He heaved a sigh. "I have cancer. It's Stage 4. And it's everywhere. And there's not a whole lot they can do."

My stomach dropped. My legs gave out. He caught me before I fell, moved me over to the wicker couch. Everything he said after that—details, how he first felt off, how long it'd been going on—sounded muffled and fuzzy, barely audible over the loud ringing in my ears, and then I sobbed against him, feeling his incredible warmth.

He just held me and didn't offer much more.

"I know, baby." He tightened his arms around me. "I know."

After a while, I was drained and went still. He said nothing. We sat. The sun began to set behind the Mount Hope Bridge.

This was going to be excruciating. Everett was going to be in pain. Everett was going to suffer. For God knew how long. Sure, they had given him only so many months, but sometimes, when the soul was strong, it forced the deteriorating body to keep going. I could take it. I could. I had to. I didn't want to be without him. I had to have him in my life for as long as possible. *We should both quit our jobs. Spend every day together.* I could steel myself. I could watch what I had to watch.

What was my other choice?

The larding needle.

It was still under the bed.

I was the new *nositel*. The new Bringer. And I needed to accept it.

End it now. End it now so he won't have to be in pain and suffer. End it now so you won't have to watch that.

A moth landed on the lip of my wine glass.

Its wings looked like a dead leaf.

The next afternoon, I knew everything I needed to, just like Nana had said. I went into the cigar box and got the three vials—they were the poisons, God knew their names, ancient concoctions from her village. I knew how much to soak the bacon in; I knew the blend for the pickling spice and what to do with the cheesecloth; I knew how much water to use to dilute the vinegar; I knew how to sear the meat to perfection.

It was like I'd been doing it my whole life.

It took me a while to get the hang of threading the raw bacon through the meat because I was madly driven to *twist in* and *weave out*, which was damn near impossible, and I recalled Nana's thick hands. I wondered if the constant work of this when she was young had perhaps made them what they were because the muscles in my lower arms and wrists were smarting by the time I was done. There were still the dumplings to make, but the thought of any more handwork was agonizing.

I decided to do those later.

For hours, the sauerbraten simmered. The sharp smell of pickling spice and bacon overwhelmed the scent of my burning black currant candles. I bundled up in Everett's olive hoodie and jeans, poured myself a glass of Nobilo, and sat on our back deck. The surface of the bay was void of recreational boats. The trees were almost free of leaves. The few souls that remained seemed to cling to their branches in staunch refusal.

I looked at my watch. Everett would be home in a couple of hours, but the sauerbraten was almost done.

I went inside and set the dining room table with our wedding china: two places, an even number. I sat in Everett's chair and had a good cry. Outside, the mourning doves cried, too.

True love isn't selfish. Sometimes it means ending the suffering no matter how much you will miss him.

I stared at Everett's empty bowl. I thought about crochet hooks and stuffed crepes, *I will love you a second time, too!* and Nana's mysterious groom. I thought of the weeping woman in Nana's village and Kučeřík, poking out his eyes. I thought about Everett, and our wedding day, and wine and sunsets behind the Mount Hope Bridge, and feeling safe; I thought about how he'd leave me and the day his warm body would grow cold; I thought about his heartbeat, his comforting smell, and how empty the house was going to be without him, and how empty my *life* was going to be without him.

How empty my life was going to be without them *both*.

I took the bowl into the kitchen and set it on the counter next to the stove. I clutched the silver ladle, filled the bowl, and ate as fast as I could.

≫≫⟩ **RECIPE** ⟨≪≪
Nana's Sauerbraten

Take three pieces of bacon and put them in a stock pot. Brown the bacon in the stock pot.

Tie strips of raw bacon on the end of a knitting needle and weave through beef (pot roast), venison, or other available meat.

Sear and brown meat in stock pot in bacon grease.

Grate and add to browned meat:
- 2 carrots
- 2 celery roots
- 1 large onion
- 1 parsley root

Add 1 part red wine vinegar to 3 parts water until it covers the meat.

Season with:
- Salt
- Pepper
- Sugar
- Pickling spice (wrapped in cheesecloth or bag)

When meat is tender, remove meat and let rest. Strain vegetables.

Remove cloth/bag of pickling spices.

Allow gravy mixture left in stock pot to cool.

Thicken gravy with 1 measure sour cream, mixed with corn starch.

Slice meat into gravy, and serve with dumplings.

Dumplings

Cube a ½ loaf of bread into small pieces and toast in the oven on low heat until dry.

Into a large bowl sift:
- 4 cups flour

Add:
- 2 whole eggs
- Salt

Beat batter until smooth.

Add:
- Cubed, dried bread

Shape into balls with floured hands.
Drop into salted boiling water.
Boil covered about 10 to 15 minutes.

Killer Lasagna

D.M. Slate

Ava held the phone between her shoulder and her ear as she stood on her tippy toes trying to reach the can of tomato paste from the top shelf of the cupboard.

Her voice was bubbly with excitement.

"I can't believe that we're finally going to meet in person. Facetime is one thing—but seeing each other in real-life is going to be amazing. I promise that the long drive will be worth it."

Chance chuckled. "It better be. You've cost me two full tanks of gas and half of my day already."

Ava's smile broadened.

"Well, buddy, if we're adding things up, I've spent a few bucks, too. I know how much you like Italian food . . . so I'm going to make you a *killer* lasagna that you won't ever forget."

"Hum. I'm surprised that they even let the 'star long-distance runner' on the track team eat lasagna?"

"Ha! They can't tell me what to eat. As long as I stay fast, that's all that matters. And besides, I *love* cooking. Almost as much as I love chemistry."

Yeah, I know, Brainiac. My GPS puts me at your house in one hour and seventeen minutes. Is my lasagna going to be done by then?"

Ava felt her eyes grow wide in shock. "Really?" she asked.

Through broken laughter, they said their goodbyes.

Ava checked the clock. One hour and fifteen minutes left.

Plenty of time.

After setting the oven to three hundred fifty degrees, she reached into the cabinet for several jars of spices and placed those onto the counter with her other supplies. Pushing a stack of chemistry textbooks aside, she cleared a spot on her small kitchen countertop.

One more week, and I'm DONE with finals. Thank God.

Walking over to her kitchen table, which also served as a desk and an entertainment console, Ava flipped on the TV to channel nine. The introduction music to Dateline was just starting.

I've been waiting for weeks to watch this episode!

She reached up into her mass of curly light-brown hair and pulled the afro of locks back into a tight ponytail.

Ava removed a sauté pan and a large pasta pan from the cabinet, placing them on the stove. After washing her hands, she filled the pasta pot with hot water, added lasagna noodles, and turned the knob to *boil*. She dumped a container of ground beef into the sauté pan and stirred the meat around as it cooked.

As the beef began to brown, her attention shifted back to the television. The host of Dateline appeared standing next to the University of Northern Colorado student center.

Butterflies stirred in her stomach.

My school.

He spoke in a monotone voice, telling viewers that Greeley, Colorado was a "quaint, home-town community with a population of just over one-hundred thousand. A city that felt safe, until nine months ago . . . "

Looking away from the TV, Ava threw a dash of seasonings into the meat: onion powder, garlic salt, pepper, and Italian seasoning. After stirring, she removed a morsel with her spoon, blowing away the steam.

Cautiously she took a bite.

Perfect.

She placed a lid onto the pan and then lifted the saucepan to drain the grease. Once back on the stove, Ava reduced the heat to *low*, looking up to the TV once again.

The host was wrapping up his narrative.

"Five young, healthy men—all found dead inside of their own burning vehicles, within nine short months. And the only common connection between them? The location of their remains, Greeley, Colorado, which is where we begin our investigation this evening for an undercover *Arson Assassin*."

Ava found herself giggling at the pun, despite the seriousness of the situation.

She grabbed the can opener and emptied a can of tomato paste and a can of tomato sauce into her meat mixture, stirring the thick goop with pleasure.

Reaching back, she flicked the knob to *off* and slid the boiling noodles onto an unused burner to cool. Ava's attention then shifted to the meat sauce, where she added another round of seasonings: salt, pepper, onion powder, garlic salt, and Italian seasoning. And for a hint of sweetness, she grabbed the bag of sugar, dumping a slight pour out of the bag before stirring the mixture together.

After placing a lid on the pan, she set the sauce to a low simmer.

Her attention was now drawn to the TV screen. The photo of a smiling young man standing in a hayfield caused her heart to freeze mid-beat. Ava felt a twinge of sadness for him.

"Arnold Jacob Smith, a twenty-three-year-old Nebraska native, was the first victim discovered in this mysterious trail of deception. His lifeless body was spotted in the burnt remains of his Chevrolet pickup in the early morning hours of August twenty-third. Local police were baffled by this horrendous crime in their seemingly safe community. To date, no persons of interest have been named in this case, and the family of Arnold Smith is desperate for answers."

The program transitioned to a commercial.

Utilizing the break in the show, Ava grabbed the pasta pot and dumped the contents into the strainer in the sink. A billowy cloud of hot steam rose up toward her face as the water rushed down the drain.

She bent down, looking in the lower cupboard for a mixing bowl. Ava grabbed a medium-sized container and placed it on the countertop. Knowing the recipe by heart, she opened the refrigerator and removed the ricotta and cottage cheeses, grated parmesan, and shredded mozzarella. Then she reached back in one more time to grab an egg before using her muscular butt-cheek to thrust the fridge door closed.

Cracking the egg into the bowl, she tossed the empty shell into the trash can. Ava reached into the drawer and removed a spoon. She scooped out half of the cottage cheese and half of the ricotta into the bowl before returning those containers to the refrigerator. She sprinkled more sugar from the bag onto the mixture. Then came the parmesan.

There's no such thing as "too much" parmesan.

Dumping a generous amount into the bowl, Ava smiled with satisfaction.

Dateline was back on.

"The second body to be identified would be that of twenty-six-year-old Marcus Johnston, a budding musician from Las Vegas. He was found just thirty-seven days after the discovery of Arnold Smith's remains and only nine miles away."

Ava looked down at the mixture in the bowl.

Something's missing.

Parsley.

Grabbing the spice from the cabinet, she gave several shakes, sending green flakes flying into the white cheese mixture. After stirring, she nodded with a satisfied smile.

"Greeley Police suspected that the cases were connected, but they could find no solid evidence to link the murders together. Not until the third young man's seared Honda was found—Jose Velasquez from Arizona—did authorities acknowledge that a serial killer was lurking within the city limits."

Goosebumps raced down Ava's arms, and she shivered.

She grabbed a rectangular glass baking dish and misted the bottom and sides with cooking spray. Then Ava began to layer: lasagna noodles, cheese mixture, meat sauce, shredded mozzarella cheese, and repeat.

Beautiful.

Placing the pan into the oven, she set the timer for thirty minutes.

Ava began to put her cooking supplies away, and she watched the TV over her shoulder.

"By now, the FBI knew about the murders, and they dispatched a team of their own to assist the local authorities in their investigation. And not long after the FBI arrived, the fourth burned vehicle would be spotted, containing the charred remains of Jamal Kirby."

Her phone began to ring, and Ava grabbed it from the counter, seeing that it was Chance. She answered with a sly smirk.

"Did you miss me already?"

He snickered. "Yeah, something like that. I had to stop for a few minutes to stretch, so I thought I'd check on my lasagna."

"Oh, I see how it is." She glanced at the stove. "It's got twenty-six minutes to go."

"Good. I should be there in half an hour. I forgot to turn the heat lamp *on* for my snake cage, so I'm going to call Grant and have him do that for me, then I'll be back on the road."

"Ahhh, good ol' Grant. He's such a helpful roommate."

Chance scoffed at the comment. "I can't stand that dude, and you know it."

Ava giggled. "Where did you tell him you were going?"

"To South Dakota to visit family."

"Nice." Her smile widened. "Alright, well, call Grant and then see me soon. Drive careful."

Chance said goodbye, and Ava hung up the phone.

Her stomach jittered with excitement and nervous energy. Ava took a deep breath, trying to calm herself. After a slow exhale, her eyes drifted back to the TV.

"The fifth victim, and most recently deceased, is nineteen-year-old Mason McGlothlin. He was an accelerated student at the University of Utah studying biochemical engineering. As a devout Mormon and member of the LDS church, Mason had strong ties with his family and community members. Detectives are actively seeking information regarding the nature of Mason's visit to Colorado. His family and friends are unaware of why he made this fatal journey."

A photo of the beaming young man in his high-school graduation gown appeared on the screen.

Ava grimaced. She shook her head slightly, trying to erase the memory.

$C_{21}H_{22}N_2O_2$. *Strychnine. That was a bad way to go.*

She'd expected violent muscle spasms, but the horror Ava witnessed that night would be carved into her brain for eternity. Strychnine was a chemical compound that she wouldn't be experimenting with again any time soon.

Reaching into the cupboard, Ava removed two opaque glass plates, one tinted pink and the other tinted blue. She set them gently onto the countertop.

No reason to take unnecessary risks.

The lasagna wasn't finished yet, so Ava took the opportunity to pick her running outfit. Making her way to the bedroom, she hummed under her breath. The soon-to-be college graduate opened her drawer, carefully selecting a pair of leggings and matching tank-top/sports bra combo. Then she retrieved her trusty practice shoes from the closet and set everything in a neat pile.

Tomorrow's run would be fourteen miles. She'd need it to burn off all of the calories in this lasagna.

Double-checking her makeup in the mirror, Ava batted her eyes and gave herself an innocent smile.

Amazing.

The timer on the oven began to *beep,* so Ava walked back to the kitchen and turned the oven off. She slid her hand into an oven mitt and removed the pan, placing it on the stovetop to cool.

$C_{12}H_{14}CI_2N_2$. *Paraquat Dichloride—tonight's secret ingredient.*

Ava removed a small vial from her purse and held it up to the light, looking through the glass at the liquid inside. Carefully, she placed the vial on the countertop.

Using a square spatula, Ava sliced the lasagna and removed a portion, placing it on the blue plate. She then removed another piece, placing it on the pink plate. Ava unscrewed the vial and used the spatula to lift the top layer of noodles and filling from the lasagna on the Chance's plate. She dribbled the liquid over the melted cheese before replacing the top half of the lasagna.

Satisfied, Ava slid the vial back into her purse.

Just as she dropped the spatula into the sink, Ava heard the *knock* at her door.

Perfect timing.

Killer Lasagna

1 pound ground beef or Italian sausage
6-8 lasagna noodles
1 can tomato sauce
1 can tomato paste
1 egg
8 oz small curd cottage cheese
8 oz ricotta cheese
½ cup grated parmesan
2 cups shredded mozzarella cheese
3 tablespoons sugar
salt
pepper
garlic salt
onion powder
Italian seasoning
parsley

Preheat oven to 350°F degrees.

Boil noodles, then drain and let cool.

Brown meat, adding salt, pepper, garlic salt, onion powder, and Italian seasoning. Drain the grease from the cooked meat, then add the cans of tomato paste and tomato sauce. Stir over low heat, then add 2 tablespoons of sugar and another round of the same spices. Cover, and let simmer for 5 minutes.

In a medium mixing bowl, combine the egg,

cottage cheese, ricotta cheese, 1 tablespoon of sugar, parsley, and grated parmesan.

Spray pan with no-stick cooking spray. Place 3-4 noodles in the bottom of the pan, then cover with ½ of the cheese mixture. Spread evenly over the noodles. Then add ½ of the meat sauce and spread evenly. Top with 1 cup of shredded mozzarella. Repeat with another layer, ending with shredded cheese.

Bake for 30 minutes and enjoy.

Sour Dough

Kate Tyte

Three months after we inherited Millford House from Pete's uncle, we rented a transit van, packed up our things, and headed south. We left the motorway and drove down smoothly-surfaced winding roads. Enormous hedgerows narrowed down the world to a suffocating green tunnel frothing with flowers. At intervals, the hedgerows dropped away, and we passed through villages where jewel-coloured flowers rampaged in the front gardens of houses that were so old they looked like they'd mushroomed up out of the earth. Signs for "The Cricketers' Arms" and "The Saracen's Head" creaked on their chains, and the front doors gleamed in the same few shades: green-ish, blue-ish, or grey-ish.

"Do you think the mortgages come with a colour chart?" I asked.

Pete laughed. "Farrow and Ball," he said. I didn't know what that meant, so I shut up and watched the scenery. This was the England they showed in the movies. It was like a foreign country.

In the afternoon, we arrived at Little Ford and parked outside Millford House. The house was a square biscuit-coloured box with four neat, regular windows on each side. The lane passed by the side of it and disappeared under a river. The first time I saw it, I thought there'd been an earthquake or something, but Pete explained that it was the "ford" in Little Ford. In the old days, they literally couldn't be bothered to build a bridge, so you just had to drive through the river, and now it was a historic feature, so they still hadn't built a bridge. Clouds of insects hovered around the edge of the water, and long ropes of bright green weed floated downriver. Behind the house, it was just fields full of cows.

Pete's parents were waiting for us. His dad grabbed one of my big plastic bags.

"What's all this?" he asked.

"Coat hangers," I replied.

"Cooowwwt hang-guuurs," he said, imitating my accent.

I felt the blood rising to my face, but Pete caught my eye and gave a barely perceptible shake of the head.

"I shouldn't think you'd be needing any coat hangers dear," said Maureen, emphasising the correct pronunciation, vowel sounds clipped into nothing, the 'g' barely perceptible, the 'er' truncated into a tiny sigh. "There'll be lots of the house."

She meant uncle John's old things, but I wasn't going to keep any of that.

"I wasn't sure what we'd need, so I've brought everything," I said.

"I can see that," said Maureen. "Let's leave the

men to it and put the kettle on. I expect you're gasping. I've made sandwiches. They've got some lovely sourdough bread now up at the beehive café. They make it themselves. They gave me some of this starter stuff; I'm going to try baking my own. And I got you some of those oaty crackers you like, they say suitable for coeliacs."

"Thanks, Maureen." I was startled to feel tears pricking behind my eyes. I thought she'd forgotten.

It was a beautiful day, so we took our food outside near the overgrown shed. I sat down on a large, round stone with a hole in the centre. I ran my hand over its grooved surface.

"What was this, originally?" I asked.

"It's the old millstone," said Pete's dad. "You know, for grinding the wheat. The river was deeper back then . . . " He droned on with his local history lesson. I held my hand in my lap like a poisonous spider and concentrated on counting my breaths to push down the anxiety. That stone had been covered in flour for centuries and centuries, and I'd rubbed my stupid hand all over it. I was dumb, I really was. Why hadn't I realised that Millford House was a flour mill? We'd have to get rid of everything. There would be flour, ancient flour, seeping out of the walls.

"Holly," Pete said, "why don't we make some more tea?" He steered me into the bathroom, where I washed my shaking hands.

"Nice slow breaths, remember," he said.

When we'd done as much as we could at the house, we walked up to The Royal Oak. The day was oozing into evening, our shadows stretching out on the road before us like they were eager to get there first. I made an excuse and went to the toilets. I needed to check that I didn't need a door key and they weren't out of order or anything, so I wouldn't get caught out. When I got back to the table, I scanned the menu: cod and chips, chicken and chips, vegetable lasagne. I went to the bar to place the orders myself: better safe than sorry.

"I'll have the salad please, but no croutons and no dressing." The woman behind the bar raised her eyebrows. Well, you can't trust chips— sometimes they're coated in flour—you can't trust chicken, and you definitely can't trust dressing. You can ask, but you can't trust the answers, and it's not really worth the trouble.

It took them seven years to diagnose me. Seven years of agonising stomach cramps and humiliating dashes to the toilet, and people mouthing "IBS" and rolling their eyes. One time the girls at work gave me a roll of toilet paper for Secret Santa. I laughed weakly, but the next day I started looking for a new job. When I was bad in hospital, down to six and a half stone, mouth ulcers seeping, horrible red sores all over, drip in my arm, I overheard auntie Linda telling mum I was anorexic. She said I was punishing mum because she never breastfed me. I was terrified of dying, but even my own family thought I was making it up. I might have died if it had gone on any longer. I imagined all my insides gushing out of me, on and on, not stopping until there was nothing left of me but a deflated bag of dried up skin.

A large glass of white appeared in front of me. I poked at my lettuce while they all stuffed themselves.

"You will be careful, won't you, Peter, now that you're working in Bristol? Only I do worry."

"Worry about what?" I asked.

"Bombers, dear. They're not going to blow anything up in Birmingham, are they? All their relatives live there. But anything could happen in *Bristol*."

I lifted my glass to my mouth and tipped it all the way back. It was empty.

"I'll be careful, mum, I promise," said Pete.

After his parents left, Pete went to the bar and returned with a whole bottle.

"They mean well," he said, squeezing my hand.

When we left the pub, the air was cool, and I was engulfed in shimmering drunkenness. Twilight bleached the colour out of everything. There was no sound except the rushing of the river.

"Let's cut across the fields," I said.

"You'll ruin your shoes," he warned.

"I'll get wellies," I said. I leaned in close to his ear and whispered, "really tight ones, Pete, so tight you'll have to ease them off me." The thought of me, in wellies, made me cackle out loud, and I ran over the grass, stumbling over long tufts and squelching through cow-pats. Pete ran after me, laughing.

"You've gone the full country bumpkin!" he called.

I pushed through the gate in the hedge and waited for him. Some living thing scuttled away from me into the undergrowth. We kissed over the top of the gate, and I pushed my tongue into his mouth.

"You're drunk," he said.

I took his hand and pushed it under my skirt, inside my knickers, to touch my smooth cleft. "I'm going to grow a big hairy bush and stop shaving my legs. Then you'll be sorry you brought me to the middle of nowhere."

"Oh, Holly," he said, in his soothing-exasperated tone, "you know I'm not bothered by all that. I love you just like you are."

"Let's do it out here," I said. "No one will see." I pushed my hands up under his T-shirt, and we kissed some more. I pulled the gate open and let him pass.

"You lie down on the grass, and I'll get on top."

"What? Why's it me who has to lie on the ground?"

"Because I'm going to be the queen of Little Ford, and you're just a peasant, you know?"

I got my own way, as usual. When we set off down the hill again, I stumbled once and nearly fell, and he steadied me. "Did ever you think," I said, "when you were a baby, that one day you'd come back and do it in the bushes with a girl like me?"

The next morning, fuzzy with my hangover, I decided to stop drinking. I wanted to start the next stage of my life as soon as possible. Why wait, I thought. I threw away my pills. I started on vitamins, but I had to go to the doctor's to get my folic acid prescribed. He raised his eyebrows when I told him I needed five milligrams a day because of my gluten-free diet, so I pushed a leaflet from the coeliac support society over the table at him. Doctors can be difficult. They don't like to acknowledge that the patients are the real experts.

Then I told myself I was living the dream. I saw my husband off to work every day with a naughty note hidden in his jacket pocket and messaged him pictures of lingerie peeping out of the bag, with promises that he'd see more as soon as he got home. At the end of the month, I was late. My breasts ached. I felt all swollen up. I was so happy I went about humming all the time. I bought pregnancy magazines. I scrolled through images of nurseries. On day thirty-four—I waited like a good girl—I peed on the stick. Negative. I couldn't believe it. Soon afterward, I started bleeding. I curled up on the bathroom floor and cried. Pete hugged me and said, "next month." I got off the floor and started cleaning again. I knew it was irrational, but I couldn't help thinking that if Millford House was contaminated with flour, I might not get pregnant. I'm paranoid, I told myself, and in the same breath, you can't be too careful.

Pete and I did our bit to integrate into the village. We dutifully went to fundraising quizzes and things at the village hall, where everybody stuffed themselves with homemade cake. Sometimes people said, "gluten-free," and looked very pleased as they pushed their offerings towards me. I nodded and smiled and took the cakes home for Pete. People get offended if you explain the risk of cross-contamination. I'd worried that going home to the village might be bad for Pete, that he might creep back into the shell I'd spent so long coaxing him out of. But all that home baking really fattened him up, and as his belly swelled, he got more assertive and made jokes about being the sole breadwinner of Millford House, as though self-confidence was simply a case of entering the room stomach-first. I felt cheated out of all that effort I'd put into telling him he was good enough. And I was jealous. If only my belly would ripen like that.

I started going to church on Sundays, hoping to fit in. I liked the cool, musty smell, the tuneless droning hymns, and the cocooning sense of centuries of tradition bearing down on me. "Give us this day our daily bread," I murmured, along with Maureen and a handful of dutiful families. When we prayed, I felt a great surge of longing and imagined my future children tumbling about on the lawn on a nice new swing set. I could picture their chubby little bodies, the softness of their hair, snuggling up in their nice, clean, warm beds, with a room each. Each month I watched for signs and I would think—this is it! But then I'd be wiping blood off myself, same as usual, and empty desolation would sweep over me.

One day Pete strolled back from his mum's place with a pot of goo. "I'm going to start making my own," he said.

"Making your own what?"

"Sourdough, of course."

I was so angry I could hardly speak. I'd spent years educating him about my health problems.

"Why keep on buying bread for toast and sandwiches when homemade is so good? And the crust is so delicious. You really have to chew it. It's good for your gut health, all that chewing."

"Good for *your* gut health," I said. "What if I get contaminated?"

"Oh, Holly! We've been over this before. Gluten doesn't fly through the air, you know. I'll use the shed out the back. I'm going to convert it into a separate kitchen. I'm thinking of getting a proper pizza oven. And maybe a really good barbecue."

"A man kitchen?" I said.

"Exactly."

"Alright," I said, relieved he hadn't gone totally crazy. "But you have to be really careful not to bring any flour inside."

The next day was Sunday. I sat on the hard wooden pew next to Maureen and thought, by the winter I'll be too big to squeeze in here. By the spring, I will be two people. We'll have a christening, I thought. Our baby deserves to have roots. Maybe I should be christened too. Then we can really belong here. After the service, I hung around the church door in the damp breeze until everyone had left.

"Reverend Greenfield?" I asked. "How do I become a part of the church, like really a part?"

He started mumbling something about doing a

course, said I could look it up on the Church's webpage. I think he wanted to get back for his lunch.

"What about communion?" I asked. "Could I do that? Only the thing is, I have to have gluten-free."

He gave a bark of laughter as though I'd asked if dogs can go to heaven.

"We many are one bread, one body: for we all are partakers in that one bread," he said. "1 Corinthians 10:17."

"But it's just symbolic, isn't it?"

"It's a slippery slope," he said. "Soon it'll be Ribena for the alcoholics and individual plastic cups for hygiene reasons. We're a traditional village church. Where's the dignity in that?"

"There's not much dignity in me sitting on the toilet for hours either, father," I said.

He drew in his cheeks like he was sucking a lemon and walked away.

"Man shall not live by bread alone!" I said desperately at his black retreating back.

Summer faded into autumn and still, there was no baby. One of the church mums had a big round belly—how hadn't I noticed it before? It wasn't fair, I thought. She already had two little ones, one in a pushchair, one clinging to her legs. The toddler took a step towards me, waving a soggy, half-chewed biscuit in his little starfish hands. I suppressed a gasp and took a step back.

She gave me a strange look and said, "Now

Tristan, you don't want to spoil Holly's nice clothes, do you?"

I bought an ovulation prediction kit and started taking my temperature. It took all the fun out of it. Pete started giving me heavy sighs and spending more time in his man kitchen. I'd tell him, "I'm ovulating, we can't miss this chance," and make him shower properly in the downstairs bathroom and clean his teeth, just in case, before we did it.

The cause of coeliac disease was discovered during the Dutch famine. During the winter of 1944-1945, the Germans cut off supplies of fuel and food to towns in the Netherlands. They called it the Hungerwinter. The canals and rivers froze. In Amsterdam, the rations dropped to 580 calories a day. The black market ran out of food. The rations dropped to one kilo of potatoes and 400g of bread a week. The gas and electricity were turned off. Four and a half million starving people prayed as one: give us this day our daily bread. They dug up the tulip bulbs and ate them. Twenty thousand people died of hunger. The elderly died, and the children died, all except in one place. In the coeliac ward of the Juliana Children's Hospital, the death rate dropped from 35 percent to zero. There were photographs of them. Before: the skin stretched thin over their distended bellies, rising up beneath the undulating wings of their rib cages, skin crusted with angry red blisters, skeleton limbs like an afterthought, glazed eyes. After: skinny babies. For coeliacs, starvation is better than bread.

During the winter, Maureen helped me hang some heavy curtains to keep the cold draughts out. As she left, she extended her face towards me. Was it my imagination, or was her face plumper, doughier? I moved to kiss her, but she had a smear of white powder on her cheek. Was it flour? With all the bread she'd been eating, it could be. I turned my head sharply, and the kiss became an awkward hug. The minute the door closed, I ran to the bathroom, turned on the shower, peeled off my clothes, and shoved them in the washing machine straight away.

One Saturday, I heard the slow, artificial jangle of the teddy bears picnic tune coming from outside. "If you go down to the woods today, you're sure of a big surprise . . . " I'd never understood why they chose that jingle; it was so sinister, like an advert for paedophiles luring kids into the woods.

"Ice-cream van, out here, in winter?" I said. I was already imagining laughing to my kids about the creepy music as they rushed out to buy ice cream. It was nice, that some things didn't change, that we'd have that connection.

"It's Ed the Bread," said Pete.

"What?"

"You know, he delivers. Like a milkman but with bread. Got any change?" Pete rummaged in the china swan on the dresser, fished out a few coins, and dashed outside. He pulled on his wellies and waded across the ford. I watched through the window. Lots of our neighbours were out there standing in line, laughing and shoving bread rolls in their mouths. After a while, Pete came to the front door cradling a round, flat loaf to his chest. It was the kind of hand-made bread that had flour all over the outside. I could smell the tangy, yeasty stink of it, even through the door. I missed the old days when bread was white and sliced and sealed in a plastic bag and didn't smell of anything. I motioned to him and said, "Go round the back."

"Don't be silly." He reached for the door, but I put the chain on. "There's flour all over that," I said. "Go round the back. Bread stays in your own kitchen."

Peter sighed as though I was being unreasonable and slumped off round the side of the house like a teenager. The house was my safe space, my only safe space. Why couldn't he respect that? He'd gotten worse since we came down here. I suppose the country is so dirty, he was falling back into bad habits. Maureen's house was often in a state—dog hair and muck all over. "Good clean dirt," she would say, approvingly. Why did he need more bread, anyway? He ate so much of the stuff. I'd have to talk to him about the size of his belly.

When spring finally arrived, I was exhausted. I had to sit down and rest halfway up the stairs. When I opened the window, I could smell the constant pub carpet stink of Pete's bread kitchen, slurry on the fields from far off, and the faint metallic tang of petrol from the main road. An acute sense of smell is one of the signs, I thought. Maybe I was finally pregnant. I cradled the secret knowledge gently to myself like a precious egg. If I shared this, even with Pete, it might break the spell, that trembling, tenuous bond. This secret was just between the two of us: me and the microscopic ball of rapidly dividing cells I hoped I carried inside.

That night I was full of nervous anticipation. It felt different from all the other months. I was half-asleep when I heard the soft, snuffling sighs and gentle breathing of a sleepy little creature. I wandered after it. There was something in the airing cupboard. I could smell it. It had the scent of a childhood camping trip, crushed grass, my brother wiggling about in his sleeping bag, his innocent baby animal smell, my parents drinking beer and murmuring outside by the fire. "Mummy . . . mummy," it whispered, "I want cuddles." I reached into the cupboard and pulled out a basket and held it in my arms. "Mummy's here," I mumbled. The soft, pliable little form shifted under its cloth and settled cosily. Reassured it was safe, I went back to sleep.

I woke up early. Sunlight was pouring in through the window. Pete's side of the bed was empty. It was May Day, the morning of the village fete. I'd suggested a face-painting stand for the kiddies, then immediately regretted it because spending all day surrounded by toddlers was bound to be painful. I needed to go to the supermarket to get some supplies and stock up on a bit of food. But something was wrong. It was the smell. Everything was permeated with a warm, yeasty smell. I wondered if it was real or if I was still dreaming. I could hear Pete moving about downstairs in the kitchen. That's nice, I thought. Breakfast. I waited for a few minutes. The constant stench of bread would be smothered by the smell of coffee any second now. I rubbed my eyes and noticed that my fingertips had some kind of beige residue on them. I rubbed them clean. There was an unpleasant noise coming from the kitchen: scrape, slap, scrape, slap. What was he doing down there? Why did it smell so bread-like? Well, I couldn't lie in bed forever. I got up and got dressed and went to the bathroom, where I quickly did my face and put my hair in a ponytail. That would have to do. I went down to the kitchen. Scrape, slap, scrape, slap. Pete was kneading bread on the counter. I staggered back. I clung to the doorframe, shaking and gasping for breath. I put my hands over my mouth.

"What are you doing?" I said.

"Bread," he said.

"But this is the *safe* kitchen!"

"Oh, Holly! It's a lovely sourdough. It's not *poisonous*."

"It is to me!" I turned my back on him and fought back my tears. My strange dream . . . was it just a dream? I turned to look at Pete, contentedly kneading dough, flour over every surface, and doubt nagged at me. "Pete . . . you're not putting dough in the airing cupboard, are you?"

Pete shrugged. I went upstairs again. Slowly, slowly. My heart was pounding. The stairs seemed to go on forever. I took a deep breath and snatched open the door. The towels and sheets had all been pushed to the back, and stacked up around the boiler were basket after basket of cloth-covered dough. A wild, stabbing pain shot through my chest. I turned and went downstairs again, leaning heavily on the bannisters. I stood in the kitchen doorway. Pete was humming gently as he went on with the bread: scrape, slap, scrape, slap.

"I don't know why you're doing this," I said, keeping my voice even, "but I want it all gone, all of it, and I want this kitchen bleached everywhere, the insides of the cupboards, everything. And the airing cupboard too. Everything goes back to your outside kitchen, everything that's had flour on it. Listen, I'm going out now, and I want everything cleaned up before I get back."

"Mmm-hmm."

"Pete! I'm serious."

"Alright, Holly. Alright."

I stood there uncertainly for a moment longer. He didn't seem concerned at all. He's gone crazy, I said to myself. Then I wondered if I was crazy. Or maybe this was his way of saying he wanted a divorce. Each explanation seemed more horrifying than the last. I was on the point of asking him, but I decided I didn't want to know, not now. When I get home, I said to myself, all this will have gone away. We can pretend it was all just a bad dream.

I parked my car and took a small trolley. "Excuse me," I said. There was a woman coming out of the supermarket, blocking my path. Her trolley was completely full of bread. Rolls, baguettes, long loaves, round loaves, loaves with seeds and without, all different colours and sizes and shapes. She was holding a baguette in her hand, and she'd bitten the end off, and she was chewing on the thick crust. Her toddler threw its head back and wailed. The woman broke off a piece of bread and stuffed it into the child's mouth. The child's jaws started to grind mechanically. I shuddered.

As soon as the automatic doors opened, I was hit by the smell of bread. They pump a chemical bread smell out around supermarkets to make people feel hungry and want to spend more. Everywhere I went, I was reminded that I was an outsider, that the things that made other people salivate made me tense with anxiety. I walked past the magazines and flowers and cards, past the huge bakery section with its banner saying, "Try Our New Sourdough," to the free-from area at the back of the shop. There was another woman there, hunched over nervously, peering at labels. I looked for my usual things: oat biscuits, rice crackers, gluten-free cereal and pasta. But everything looked different. There were all sorts of packet bread mixes there. I picked one up and looked at the label. It was made of wheat flour; it wasn't gluten-free at all. I put it down quickly. There could be flour on the outside of that packet, I thought. I'd have to have a shower again when I got home. I started checking the other packets. It was all mixes for normal wheat bread. I exchanged a look with the other woman, who shrugged.

I found a member of staff. "Excuse me?" I said. "There's been a mistake with the shelf-stacking. There's lots of gluten in the free-from section. And I can't find my usual gluten-free foods."

"I'm sorry, madam. We're reorganising," he said, without looking at me.

"Where can I find my usual products, then?"

He shrugged.

A wave of exhaustion swept through me.

"Forget it," I muttered and pushed past him. I was tired, so tired of all of this. If even my own husband didn't care about poisoning me, why should the supermarket? The automatic doors parted smoothly before me as though they sensed my mood and were getting out of my way.

I got into my car, wiped my hands with several wet-wipes, and rubbed them with hand sanitiser. Then I just sat there for a moment and closed my eyes. It's ok, I told myself. I'll go to another supermarket. I'll make an official complaint. I really didn't feel well. I started going through everything I'd eaten in the last twenty-four hours, checking for anything that might not have been safe. It was probably Pete, I thought, contaminating my kitchen. Life would be easier if I just gave up, I thought, if I just ate gluten and got sick. I sank down into futility and self-pity and cried, leaning my head on the steering wheel.

When I got home, Pete was out. The house still stank of bread, and he hadn't cleaned the kitchen. It wasn't a nightmare then, it was real. After my cry, I felt scoured on the inside, empty and hollow like a carved out pumpkin. My anxiety had receded to a dull throb. My stomach was churning, and I realised I hadn't even bought myself any food or re-stocked the face paints. I packed up the things I had anyway and went over to the village green by the church. If I was contaminated, if I was going to have symptoms, there was nothing I could do now. I'd get through the day, make sure the kids had a nice time, then I'd have a serious talk with Pete. I'd tell him that this time I really might be pregnant, that it wasn't only my health on the line, but our child's.

It was strangely quiet on the green, and there weren't many stalls set out. One of the church ladies waved at me uncertainly from behind a table piled with bric-a-brac. A limp string of bunting slithered off her stand and flopped to the ground. Most people seemed to be gathered around a van parked outside the entrance to the village hall. Probably unloading things or having a briefing. I recognised Pete's back in the same too-tight, pale-blue shirt he'd had on earlier. He had flour all over him. I stood next to him, but I couldn't bring myself to touch him. I said, "Pete, you mucky pup, people will think I don't look after you!" My voice dropped in the quiet like a glass breaking in a restaurant, and the blood rushed to my cheeks. "Sorry," I whispered. Why were they so silent? Then I noticed that they weren't silent, not exactly. They were making a faint, wet, sloppy noise. I looked at Pete, but his eyes were glazed, and he didn't seem to see me. He swayed slightly. His jaws were moving rhythmically round and round.

"Pete?" I said.

He thrust his hands out, they all did, letting out a low moan of longing, and Reverend Greenfield leaned out of the van with a loaf of bread in his hand. He handed it out, and then another, then another. The villagers passed the bread amongst themselves. Pete took his loaf and sank his teeth into it and chewed.

"What's going on?" I asked. "Maureen," I said, spotting her, "you said you'd help me with face-painting, why don't we go and get set up? It's time to start."

Maureen turned to look at me. Her hair was standing up on one side, and she hadn't done her make-up. Her face was slack and pasty. "The kids don't want face-paint, Holly," she said. "They want bread." She ripped off a hunk of bread with her teeth and chewed. I looked around. Nobody looked at me. They were all chewing and chewing.

Reverend Greenfield came towards me, cradling a loaf against his chest like the baby Jesus. "We are one body, one bread," he said. He held the golden loaf out towards me in his two arms. I had a flashback to running to the bathroom, doubled up in pain.

"I can't eat bread," I said, backing away.

'We've all broken bread together, Holly," Maureen

said, thrusting a loaf at me. "Why don't you break bread with us too?"

"I can't," I said, and she lowered the bread sadly.

"Pete," I said, "I think I'm finally pregnant. Let's get away from here." I tugged on his floury arm.

"You're not one of us, Holly," he said.

He turned away from me to join the others, and they went on quietly chewing and chewing. I couldn't bear it anymore. I turned and ran. I ran across the fields, and I ran until my lungs were burning so that I had to stop. I grasped hold of the gate and doubled over with a stitch in my side. Nausea swept over me, and I vomited onto the grass. Was it morning sickness, I wondered, or was it gluten? Finally, I straightened up and wiped my mouth. This was where Pete and I had shagged on the ground, that first night in the village. That was a long time ago. The field rippled down towards Millford House and the river. It was rich and green, so green, full of beautiful new plant life, optimistic and hopeful. This field was normally just full of scrubby grass and cows. When had it changed? I looked closer. The plants had seeds at their tips nestled together like ropes of plaited hair. There was a breath of wind, and the plants bobbed their heads to me in greeting. It wasn't grass, I realised. It was wheat.

⇢⇢⇢ **RECIPE** ⇠⇠⇠

Gluten Free Sourdough Bread

3 cups Gluten Free All Purpose Flour
1/4 cups cassava flour (or buckwheat flour)
1/4 cups dry milk powder (or coconut milk powder)
1/2 tsp. baking soda
2 tsp. baking powder
1 tsp. sea salt
2 large eggs
2 Tbsp apple cider vinegar
1/4 cup olive oil
1/4 cup sugar
1 Tbsp psyllium husk powder
3/4 cup gluten free sourdough starter
1 1/4 cup club soda, sparkling water, ginger ale, 7-Up
   or naturally gluten free beer

Bring all ingredients to room temperature.

Preheat oven to 200°F.

Beat the following ingredients together in a large mixing bowl: eggs, apple cider vinegar, oil, sugar, psyllium husk powder and gluten free sourdough starter. Mix until smooth and thickened, approximately 2 minutes.

Slowly stir in dry ingredients with bubbly liquid, using a wooden spoon until the batter is smooth and all dry ingredients are completely integrated. Mix for several minutes with spoon.

Transfer dough to an oiled Pan, lightly dusted with gluten-free Flour. Dust the top of the dough with more gluten-free Flour and brush with olive oil for best results.

Cover with oiled plastic wrap and set inside oven. Turn oven off and turn light on.

Allow the dough to rise for at least 1 1/2 hours, or up to 3 hours before baking.

Preheat oven to 350°F or 325°F convection.

Remove plastic wrap and slice the top of the dough to direct the rise.

If you prefer a very crunchy crust, fill a spray bottle with water and spritz the dough before baking, and again every 15-20 minutes while baking.

Bake loaf in the pan for 75 minutes before testing with a bread thermometer. The internal temperature should reach at least 205°F before removing to cool. If the bread is browning too much, cover with foil in order to keep baking.

Once bread is fully cooked, remove to cool on a wire rack for 15 minutes before removing from the pan. Allow to fully cool before slicing.

Hell-Spawn Chicken Masala

Nidheesh Samant

I was all ready for dinner. Every month, one of us hosted the other three. As lovers of all things spicy, we had set a condition for our meals: The food was to be tongue numbingly spicy. We tried to outdo each other at every dinner. Tonight was going to be my magnum opus. My chicken masala had turned out perfect. The addition of my secret ingredient—the Hell-spawn sauce—had made the chicken volcanic. One whiff was enough to clear out the most rigid of colds.

It was only by sheer luck that I happened upon the Hell-spawn sauce. On my way back from the supermarket, I had spotted a small, obscure grocery shop. Since the supermarket had nothing new to offer, I decided to give the shop a visit. After expressing my desire for the spiciest wares available, the elderly shopkeeper had shown me the bottle of sauce. The trial whiff had been enough to effect my purchase of the sauce. The old man had warned me not to use more than a couple of drops. I was used to such warnings, usually given by people who had no stomach for the hot stuff.

Once I had reached home, I promptly ignored the warning and began prepping the chicken. I used a generous drizzle of the sauce and salivated at the thought of winning the challenge. As the bell rang, I took off my apron and rushed to open the door. There stood my three friends, grinning away. Clearly, the aroma of the chicken had wafted outside my apartment. Ben, Jamal, and Raj took their seats at the dining table and produced a bottle of Shiraz. From the hungry look on their faces, I knew there was no time to waste on pleasantries. As I began serving the chicken masala, Jamal poured out the wine. Even before I had served everyone, Raj started wolfing down his chicken. He did not stop until his bowl was clean, leaving us staring wide-eyed at our friend. Raj raised his palms.

"I guess it just wasn't spicy enough. Last week's prawns were clearly . . . "

A bout of coughing cut short Raj's words. We could see beads of sweat build upon his brow. We could not help but snigger watching Raj struggle for water. Within seconds, he had finished the bottle of water I had handed over. However, his condition only worsened. His skin turned a deep hue of red. As he got up from his chair, I could see his entire body was drenched in sweat. His veins were clearly visible now as he continued clutching his gut and coughing. Raj fell to his knees. His skin only continued getting redder. I handed him another bottle of water. I could feel the heat emanating from his body. I motioned to Ben, telling him to call the emergency services.

As Ben struggled to dial with his trembling fingers, Raj threw his head back and let out a blood-curling scream. I could see steam rising from his entire body. It was as if Raj was on fire. Ben had finally managed to contact the services, but seeing Raj's condition had knocked the words right out of his mouth. None of us could utter a word. Raj was now completely silent, staring at us with bloodshot eyes. Only the sound of his now crackling skin punctured the silence that had settled. I reached out to my friend.

"Raj? Are you okay?"

It was a stupid question because the man was clearly not fine. In fact, I wasn't sure we could call him a man anymore. His red skin, bloody eyes, hairless body, and visibly black veins stood as evidence against the claim. He looked like what he had consumed, a hell-spawn. The creature that was Raj continued staring at us, the hunger visible in its eyes. The three of us looked at each other. I gestured with my eyes, pointing in the direction of my room. We took a silent step backward. And another and another. Until we were almost at the bedroom door. The creature did not budge and continued staring at us. Jamal went inside first, followed by me. As Ben took his last step, his foot banged into the door, causing him to let out a whelp of pain.   The   creature roared. It moved swiftly across the room and grabbed Ben by his shoulders. Ben screamed in anguish as the creature's touch burnt through his clothes, searing his flesh. I tossed the jug of cold water in my bedroom at the creature's hands. With a moan, it released Ben just long enough for us to pull him inside the room and slam the door shut. We locked the door and backed away from it. The creature let out another scream as it began thumping on the door. I had noticed Ben drop his phone next to the dining table and dialed his number from my phone. As soon as it rang, the thumping on the door stopped. We could hear the creature moving towards the phone until suddenly, it went dead. I rushed to my desktop and opened the security system. The camera in the dining room displayed the creature fumbling around. By its side, lay Ben's burnt mobile phone.

Jamal laid the semi-conscious Ben on my bed. The area around his shoulders where the creature held him had turned black with a thin silver crust of skin. His flesh released a revolting smell, almost causing us to barf. As we gently poured water to soothe the burns, Ben let out a howl of pain before fainting. Angry red boils began popping up on the skin wherever his flesh was exposed to the water. Slimy white pus oozed out of the boils. We realized we needed more water to clean the wound and reduce its heat. Without water, Ben's condition would only worsen. Unluckily, it was available only in the kitchen. The creature stood between water and us. I got back to observing the security system.

The creature was shuffling around the house aimlessly. Every few minutes, it would scream, making my heart thump faster and Ben's body spasm. He needed more water, and there was none left in the bedroom. All the water was in the kitchen. I walked up to the door and nodded to Jamal. He understood my intentions. It was risky, but it was the only chance Ben had. Jamal kept his eyes trained on the monitor.

The moment the creature walked into the living room, Jamal signaled me. I opened the door and slipped out, shutting the door to safety behind me.

The creature did not notice me. It continued its meandering and moaning. I tiptoed to the dining table. My heart sank when I saw the empty bottles of water. I picked up one in each hand and continued to the kitchen sink. As I filled the bottles of water, I realized the complete silence other than the sound of flowing tap water. A hot breath of wind tickled my neck. I slowly turned around and stared into red emptiness. It looked like embers of fire, which were hungered for more fuel. I gasped. I was looking into the bloody eyes of the creature. Our faces only inches apart, the heat of the creature stung my face. As it roared, ready to take a bite at me, my instincts kicked into gear. I whipped my arms and splashed water from the bottles on its face. The creature let out another moan as its face sizzled, releasing smoke.

I rushed to the side, dodging its flaying arms. I tripped, crashing into the fridge. I ducked behind the open fridge door, avoiding the creature's next strike. The violent swing took the door clean off its hinges. Among the contents of the fridge that lay scattered on the floor, I noticed the culprit of this catastrophe. In a last-ditch attempt, I pushed myself towards the bottle. The creature was directly over me, ready to pound me into the ground with its fists. As I lay prone on my back, I reached my arms over my head. The creature's drool burnt through my clothes as it fell on me. My quivering fingers clasped the tiny glass bottle. As the creature let out a loud victorious roar, I flung the bottle into its mouth, hoping for the best.

The creature took a step back, clutching its throat. Its entire body began convulsing and shuddering. Its skin crackled even more as it began glowing crimson. A black liquid began oozing out from its eyes and mouth. Gurgling out its throes of anguish, the creature sputtered and choked as the black liquid covered its entire body, consuming it. All that remained was the pool of black liquid and a strong, rancid smell. The small glass bottle stood in the center of the slimy pool. Its contents refilled, the Hell-spawn sauce stood ready for reuse.

⫸⫸⫸ **RECIPE** ⫷⫷⫷
Hellish Chicken Masala

1 cup basmati rice
1 1/2 tbsp canola oil
1 1/2 lb boneless, skinless chicken thighs, cut into 1-inch chunks
Salt & Pepper to taste
1/2 medium yellow onion, diced
3 tbsp tomato paste
3 cloves garlic, minced
1 tbsp freshly grated ginger
1 1/2 tsp garam masala
1 1/2 tsp chili powder
1 1/2 tsp ground turmeric
1 (15-ounce) can tomato sauce
1 cup chicken stock
1/2 cup heavy cream
2 tbsp chopped fresh cilantro leaves
A bottle of your favorite hot sauce. (we at Madness Heart Press recommend the Tears of Joy—Red Fang's Night Destroyer Scorpion Pepper sauce personally)

In a large saucepan of 2 cups water, cook rice according to package instructions; set aside.

Heat canola oil in a large stockpot or Dutch oven over medium heat. Season chicken with salt and pepper, to taste. Add chicken and onion to the stockpot and cook until golden, about 4-5 minutes.

Stir in tomato paste, garlic, ginger, garam masala,

chili powder and turmeric until fragrant, about 1 minute.

Stir in tomato sauce and chicken stock; season with salt and pepper, to taste. Bring to a boil; reduce heat and simmer, stirring occasionally, until reduced and slightly thickened, about 10 minutes.

Stir in heavy cream until heated through, about 1 minute.

Serve immediately with rice, garnished with cilantro, and add as many drops of your hot sauce as you can handle, ideally without overpowering the flavors of the Masala.

Fit For The Gods

Tim Mendees

*"In Physicia Baal is still worshipped as Bolus, and
as Belly he is adored and served with abundant
sacrifice by the priests of Guttledom."*
—Ambrose Bierce.

I.

A chill, north-easterly wind rustled through the branches of the wizened old elm as the horse-drawn carriage rattled to a halt. Inspector Moore jumped down from the transport and landed with a dull splat in the thick mud.

It had been raining for what seemed like years. Winter in Cornwall is often an ordeal. Cursing to himself, he stumbled to release his boots from the sucking soil. Once free, he straightened his tie, pulled his cloak tight around his tweed suit, and gave the ends of his luxuriant moustache a twirl.

The ride from Truro to Betyls Cove had been gruelling. The rattling of metal wheels on rough, rocky roads had left him with a definite kink in his spine. He looked up at the sky with a frown. Thick dark clouds glowered down upon the crime scene, adding an extra element of the dramatic. Droplets of frigid water ran down his bulbous nose and dripped off the end, landing with a plop in the muddy pools.

Just back from the road, a huddle of blue tunics stood over what looked, from a distance, like a bundle of rags. Sergeant Poole had managed to lower himself from the police carriage with a damn sight more dignity than his superior, then rounded the vehicle and joined the Inspector.

The two veteran policemen carefully walked over to the scene, giving the worst of the mud a wide birth. A green-faced young constable by the name of Smith spotted their approach and rushed over to meet them.

"So, what have we got, Constable?" Moore asked.

"It's 'orrible, sir! Bloody 'orrible." The shaken youth began. "It's old Sam Whittington's daughter. One of the farm 'ands from the Marsh place found 'ur on the way t'work. Gutted like a fish she is, sir."

"Jesus." Sgt. Poole sighed, crossing himself.

"Has the Doc seen the body yet?" asked Moore.

"Aye, sir."

"Do we have a time of death?"

"Doc reckons she's been dead about six 'ours, sir. Though all this bloody rain makes it difficult to be sure."

"Thanks, Constable," Moore said, checking his fob-watch and mopping a mixture of sweat, rain, and last night's scotch off his brow. "Come along, Poole. Let's take a look."

Sergeant Pool gasped and held a handkerchief to

his mouth upon viewing the body. The late Miss Whittington had been ravaged. Her abdomen had been laid open with a certain degree of skill, and her intestines had been lifted from the stomach cavity. They lay next to her like a pile of sausages.

"Well?" Moore asked the shaken looking police surgeon.

"Well, what?" Dr. Turnbull waveringly replied.

"Is there . . . " Moore cleared his throat with a gentle cough. "Is there anything missing?"

"Uh, yes, both kidneys."

Moore swore under his breath and motioned to the doctor to cover the poor woman up with an old sack. As thunder rumbled in the distance, Moore stared across the hills pensively.

"Jim?" Sgt. Poole asked gently. "Is it the same?"

"Yes, Frank, I'm most afraid it is."

All Hallows' Eve, most places in Britain, brings out more than its fair share of fruitcakes: middle-aged women hosting wild sex parties, mild-mannered bankers sacrificing chickens, little Johnny Smith covering himself in feathers and gobbling like a Turkey. Betyls Cove was now very obviously the home to a much more dastardly kind of nutter, because, for the third year in a row, one of the local women had been relieved of her precious bean-shaped organs.

The first two victims had been local "unfortunates," as the Victorian euphemism went: ladies of the night, tarts, prostitutes. The removal of the kidneys had been carried out with far less precision than last night's victim. It was as though the kidney thief had been practising.

The Betyls Cove station house was alive with the scurrying and mumbling of "raw lobsters." Inspector Moore and Sargent Pool had taken command of the small briefing room, a handful of peelers and a classroom's worth of blackboards.

Dr. Turnbull had scribbled the details of all three victims' mutilations on the largest of the boards, with a rapidly diminishing stick of chalk and in a script legible only to takers of the Hippocratic oath.

All three women had been laid open from top to tail, their intestines scooped out and the kidneys removed. The first victim had been an obvious rush job, as one of the kidneys had been dropped inside the abdominal cavity and left behind. The second still had parts of the organs attached. But the third victim had been snipped neatly clear.

The killer had switched up his tool of choice with positive results. The knife used in the first two murders had been a short-bladed fishing or cobbler's knife. The fresh cadaver had been carved up with, what the doctor postulated, a butcher's boning-knife.

"Should we bring in Tom the butcher then, sir?" asked a young bobby named Jeffries.

"No need, he's here already," Poole replied. "He's been 'ere since closing time. It seems he 'ad a belly full of porter and got in a ruckus down at the Sirens Rest.

He's been sleeping it off in the cells since closing time."

"Still . . . " Moore interjected. "It might be worth asking him if he has had any knives pinched, or lent any to someone."

"Could it be 'Saucy Jack,' sir?" Jeffries asked again, much to the displeasure of Inspector Moore.

"Don't be ruddy silly, Constable!" He bellowed. "Every copper worth his salt knows he's safely banged up in bedlam."

"But the papers, sir, they said he never.." Jeffries mewled.

"The Papers!" Moore fumed. "What the bloody hell do they know? Fred Abberline says he's locked up in a nuthouse, and that's good enough for me." Inspector Moore had turned as red as a beetroot and looked as though he was going to spontaneously combust. This topic was a sore one. As a veteran of the "autumn of terror," any mention of the ripper sparked his short fuse into ignition.

Composing himself somewhat, Moore asked the room, "Anything found at the scene?"

An uncertain negative murmur spread around the room. Coppers looked at one another sheepishly and shook their heads. Moore put his hands on his hips and blew air out of his ruddy cheeks. As he started to turn away in despair, the suitably cowed voice of Jeffries piped up once more. "Well, there was the sack, sir."

"The sack?" Moore queried. "The one we covered her up with, you mean?"

"Yes, sir, we found it in the bushes," Jeffries said, brightening. He sensed a career lifeline.

"Anything to tell us where it came from?"

"Yes, sir! It's from the Stanley mill. It's written on the side."

"Good work, Jeffries," Moore said, much to the young constable's delight. He turned and scribbled "sack" on the blackboard behind him. Turning sharply like a bloodhound with the scent of iron in its nostrils, he poised to address the room.

Before he could speak, the saloon doors that separated the front desk from the briefing room clattered off the walls, and a soaking wet constable blustered into the room. "Sir! Come quick! there has been another one!"

II.

Lard sizzled in the large skillet. The scent of frying onions tickled the young man's tastebuds. A pinch of salt and a handful of finely chopped celery, carrots, garlic, and scallions were added to the pan. A gentle stir of the stock vegetables and he could return to the important task of dicing his fresh meat.

What police constable Smith forgot to mention was that the new victim wasn't human, not in the slightest.

"It's a chuffing bull!" Moore spat.

"It's not just any bull, sir," Smith replied. "It's Wilf Jones' prize breeder, sir, worth a bleedin' fortune at auction. Young Ivy was up 'ere pickin' 'urbs for 'er brother when she came across 'im."

Moore looked at Poole with a look that said 'bloody yokels' and spoke in measured tones. "I don't care if it's the pope's prize bull, constable. A woman has just been murdered, making three. Tell Sgt. Ingram that I told him to get off his lardy-backside and investigate this. I have better things to do than look into what is probably a rival farmer tipping the odds before the county show. Come along, Poole. Let's get back to the station." As he turned to walk back down the steep hill towards town, the voice of Dr. Turnbull halted him in his tracks.

"Jim, you are going to want to look at this."

Moore snapped his head around into a well-practised "this had better be good look." The doc was on his hands and knees in the cold Cornish mud, his tweeds stained with grass, mud, blood, and cow-pats. He extended a bony finger and pointed to the end of a large incision. "I've seen this mark at the end of the cut before, not three hours since." Moore and Poole looked at each other grimly. "It's of my opinion that this incision was caused by the same blade that opened up Miss Whittington. This mark is most likely caused by a crack or notch in the blade."

Moore removed his topper and ran his fingers through his steely hair. "Was anything taken?" he asked, mentally repeating the mantra, *don't say kidneys, don't say kidneys, don't say kidneys.*

"I think so. It looks as though a large portion of meat has been skilfully removed. The organs appear intact. I can't tell you for sure what cut has been taken, as my specialty isn't bovine anatomy, as I'm sure you understand, but I would say, the fillet perhaps."

"Most expensive cut, sir," Smith helpfully interjected.

"Smith," Moore began. "Get back to town and get Ingram and some of the others up here with a trolley. I want this bull taken to the morgue."

Smith gave a snappy "Sir!" and raced down the hill, slipping and sliding in the mud as he went.

"Inspector!" The doctor gave a sharp cry. "Take a look at this." As he lifted the loose flank of the beast, he pointed his skeletal finger at a dusting of white powder. "Flour," he asserted.

Flour in the wound, flour sack by the body, a name on the sack. "Come along, Poole. I think we need to talk to Mister Stanley, don't you?"

Sieve the flour, the finer, the better. The last thing you need is big gluey clumps. That's what ruined the last one. Add sea salt and crushed peppercorns to the flour, mix in the finely chopped herbs, and add the meat . . .

The Stanley mill stood alone on a stretch of the River Camel, just outside the sleepy village of High Bend. It took around thirty minutes for the carriage to navigate the flooded roads. Torrents of muddy water had burst the banks, swamping the area and dragging foul-smelling weeds onto the byway.

As the horses came to a stop and stamped their hooves in the mud, it became suddenly clear that there was "trouble at mill." Mrs. Stanley, a matronly lady with a bosom like beachballs, came hurrying towards them, waving her arms around like a whirling dervish.

"Officer, Officer!" she wailed, in a voice that would make a banshee wince. "It's my Alf. Some bugger's clobbered him!"

The two officers leapt down from the cab, covering Moore in wet filth once more, and hurried over to the cottage next to the mill proper.

Alf Stanley sat in a rocking chair with a bandage wrapped tightly around his bald head. His eyes rolled and bobbed, attempting to focus on his visitors. The local quack from High Bend mopped his brow with a wet flannel.

Moore's hopes of having a good suspect were dashed in an instant. It was clear that he had been knocked for a loop. Dr. Waite confirmed that he had been with the family since just after eleven the previous evening. So that was that—a concrete alibi.

Dr. Waite had been settling down to supper with his wife when a rigorous banging on his door made him drop his bread in his soup with a splat. It was Charlie Stanley, Alf's twelve-year-old son. He urged the doctor to "come quick" and went racing back up the road.

Slowly the story was relayed to the two stout

coppers. The wind was fierce the previous evening, and a particularly vicious gust blew the mill door open. The Stanleys were in bed, but the horrific banging of the heavy oak door on hard stone rudely awoke them.

Alf grumbled and cursed. He was filled to the brim with strong ale and pheasant, spuds, and gravy. He rolled his ample frame out of bed and groped for the oil-lamp on the bedside table. Once the room was illuminated, he pulled his slacks over his woollen long-johns and pulled on his great-coat.

The door swung in the wind as Alf approached, grumbling and belching, trying to rid himself of a painful balloon of indigestion. He grabbed the door and began to pull it closed when he was alerted by a furtive noise from within. "Hello!" he barked. Nothing answered. Alf grabbed a rusty pitchfork from next to the door and went inside. Muttering about "Damn rats!" and "Useless cats!" he swung the oil-lamp around the room. A shadow loomed upon him from behind, and a swift and powerful blow felled him like a dead oak.

When Alf hadn't returned for a disconcerting length of time, Mrs. Stanley roused Charlie and sent him to look for his pa. Charlie found his dad lying face-down in a pile of horse droppings and, for a moment, thought his distinctly rotund father had suffered a heart attack. Upon closer inspection, however, he spotted the slowly weeping duck's-egg on the back of his head and the half-brick on the floor next to him.

"Did the intruder take anything?" Poole asked the boy.

"Just a couple of sacks of flour, sir," the young boy replied.

III.

Gently brown the meat in the fat, then add the cooking liquor. Push the stock vegetables through a fine sieve, and add to the pot. Gently bring to the boil.

The young man repeated the recipe like an incantation, biting his bottom lip in anticipation.

The wind and rain hadn't let up in days. In fact, it seemed to rise to almost biblical proportions. Moore and Poole were cold, wet, miserable, and downright cheesed off by the time they got back to the station. The night was drawing in, and the fuzzy glow of the gas-lamps through the windows looked warm and inviting.

"THIS AN OUTRAGE!" a voice boomed as they entered the station. The mayor of Betyls Cove, Thomas Edwards, was a slight man with narrow eyes and a thin pencil moustache, which gave him a weasel-like appearance. He stood in the centre of the room, bellowing like an angry boar.

"What the blue blazes are going on, Ingram?" Moore yelled over the din.

"I'll tell you what's going on, Inspector!" Edwards interrupted, flecks of spit forming at the corners of his mouth. "Some scoundrel has pinched a priceless bottle of wine out of my study. It was to be a gift to

Queen Victoria herself! And this oik," he jabbed his finger at Sgt. Ingram, "says that you are too busy to catch the bounder! It's an outrage, I tell you! A BLOODY OUTRAGE!"

"Do you have any idea who took it?" Poole asked calmly.

"Isn't that your job?" Edwards blurted in response.

"LOOK!" Moore boomed, his temper reaching boiling point. "We are currently investigating a string of murders. There have been three so far . . . "

" . . . Four, sir!" Constable Smith interjected.

"WHAT!" Moore erupted.

"Four, sir. The three women and Big Jock."

"WHO the DEVIL is Big Jock?!"

"The bull, sir. He was a prize-winning Aberdeen Angus."

"SHUT UP, SMITH!" Moore snapped. "As you can see, *mister mayor,* we are up to our eyeballs in corpses at the moment, and I'm sure you don't want any more while we are out on a wild goose chase for a bottle of bloody *vin de table*!"

"Vin De Table! How dare you?" Edwards fumed.

"If you will excuse me, I have work to do. SMITH! Take the mayor's statement."

"Yes, sir!" The hurt-looking bobby replied.

Moore and Poole pushed through the throng of bemused policemen that had gathered around the fuming politician. Moore was furious. He kicked his chair against the wall and grabbed the bottle of scotch off the shelf. He turned to the picture of the Queen above his desk. "Sorry, ma'am," he toasted, "I'll find your booze when I clear this mess up." He passed the bottle to Poole, who took a welcome slug.

The two men sat down in front of the blackboards and stared at the collection of squiggles and rough sketches, desperately seeking inspiration.

Jeffries knocked on the doorframe and cleared his throat. "Sorry to bother you, sir, but I think you need to hear this." Behind him loomed the dishevelled form of Tom Drake, the town butcher and chief drunkard.

Moore motioned for both men to sit and begin. Jeffries started, while Drake sat and looked worried. "I asked Tom here about the knife like you asked and . . . "

"I didn't do anything!" Tom interrupted. "I swear, I didn't 'urt no-one."

"Easy, Tom. Relax. You couldn't have done it. You were locked up at the time." Poole reassured the butcher.

"Ahh, alright," Tom sighed. "Who'd a thought that bein' locked up 'ud be a gud thing?" He gave a nervous laugh.

"Just don't make a bloody habit of it, alright?" Moore snapped.

"Anyway, the knives, Tom, what can you tell us?" Poole continued.

"Well, I 'ad this apprentice see," Tom began. "He were great to begin with, real quick learner. Anyhow, ee started pinching meat, so I 'ad to let 'im go. Thing is, the thievin' little bugger took some of me knives when he went."

Moore's eyes lit up. "When was this?"

"Oh, a couple o' months back."

"Did you report the thefts?" Poole asked.

"Nah, I jus' reckon I'd smack him about a bit next time I saw 'im."

"So, who was this apprentice then?" Moore asked, getting the scent once more.

"That little scrote Sam Francis."

"Hang on. Francis? Why does that name ring a bell?" Moore pondered.

"It were 'is sister that found Big Jock, sir," Jeffries said.

"Right. Go and find her. I want to know what she was doing up there."

"Collectin' 'urbs, she said," Jeffries responded as he left the room.

Inspector Moore's face crumpled into a mask of concentration. The jigsaw pieces were starting to click into place, the gears were turning, the engine was pumping . . . A gas-light of inspiration went off above his head. "Tom, which cuts of meat was Sam pinching?"

"Uh, beef, fillet steak. The most expensive ruddy cut!"

Once the stew has boiled, remove from the heat, then cover and place in an oven on a moderate heat. Braise for ninety minutes or until the meat is tender and the stew thick, smooth, and rich.

The man was happy with his work. It was looking good, fit for a king, fit for a god. Next, he had to prepare the pastry.

"Sam said he'd pay me a farthin' if I went and got 'im some 'urbs," little Ivy Francis said. "He said he was making a pie fit for the gods."

"A pie?" Moore asked gently.

"Yeah, a big pie. He tried makin' it before but mucked it up."

"Thanks, Ivy, here's a lollipop. You have been a big help," Moore said, handing the girl a sweetie.

"Thanks, mister," she replied and skipped out of the station.

Moore and Poole looked at each other in disbelief. "A bloody pie?" Poole said. "Who is this kid, Sweeney Todd?"

"Let's go and bring him in," Moore said decisively.

The pie was ready. He had rolled out the pastry into a large tin. Spooned the steak and kidney filling into the pastry. Topped it, crimped it, and glazed it with a goose egg.

Nothing could go wrong now; all he had to do was bake it. He checked the oven and deemed it ready. With a sense of profound satisfaction, he slid the tin into the oven and shut the door.

There was a dribble of wine left in the bottle that he had lifted from the town hall. He savoured its complex taste. All he had ever wanted was nearly in his grasp. His lord couldn't deny this one; it was perfect. All he had to do was wait.

"Open up! Police!" Poole yelled as they banged on Sam Francis' door. Giving up, he rammed his broad shoulder against it, springing it open.

Sam's house was nothing more than a hovel, a disturbing one at that. From just a glance, it was clear that he hadn't attended church in a while. The wall was covered in charcoal symbols of distinctly diabolic and occult nature.

Poole whistled as he surveyed the room. The rickety dining table was piled high with reams of notes, letters, and journals. Sam had been a busy boy. Where he had collated all this information from was a mystery that could wait for another day.

To one side of the room was a makeshift altar. Two large candle-sticks with thick tallow candles flanked a horrific idol, carved from a strange green stone, similar to soapstone. The Idol depicted a colossal monolith topped with what looked like a gigantic, winged toad.

"Bugger me," Moore muttered under his breath. He examined the statue and barely suppressed an involuntary shudder of revulsion.

Poole had been scanning some of the papers and gave Moore a nudge. "Hey, listen to this: 'According to Eibon, if I am to wake the sleeping god, I must pay him tribute. A gift of food is the obvious choice. He is the king of gluttony, so it must be a meal fit for a god.'"

"Christ," Moore said, "when was that dated?"

"Just over two years ago. Hey, listen to this one: 'Damn it all, it wasn't perfect, not enough kidney!' That was a couple of months later, and then there is this one from last year: 'Damn it all, the whore had

Bright's disease, and the gravy had lumps in, it's no good.'"

"So, let me get this straight," Moore pondered. "This lunatic has been killing women to bake a pie for some toad-god? It just beggars belief! Come along, Frank. We need to find this nutter right now."

A piercing shriek rang out in the night. Moore and Poole burst out of the house to see a scene that blasted their minds. The town square was bustling with frenzied activity. Women and children screamed and ran; an overturned cab burned after colliding with a gas-lamp. The vicar stood on an overturned banana-box, yelling about the end of days.

Lightning flashed, and thunder rumbled as Moore and Poole stood, mouths agape. Suddenly, something large landed at Poole's feet. It was raining still, but it was no longer raining water. It was raining toads. Big, vicious toads.

The batrachian beastie that had landed in front of their very eyes was around the same size as a Yorkshire Terrier. It blinked at them malevolently through bulbous eyes; its bony ridges and taught green skin gave it an armoured, grumpy look.

Without warning, the creature sprung towards Poole with its needle-like teeth bared. Before he could shout, "Whoever heard of a toad with teeth?" Poole was fighting to keep the vicious amphibian away from his throat.

Moore whacked the toad with the butt of his revolver and helped Poole throw it clear. With a dead-eye aim, Moore let off a shot that sent the toad spinning into the bushes. Moore dusted his friend down and checked that he hadn't been bitten.

“What the hell is going on!” Poole cried hysterically.

“Hell is what’s going on, Sergeant! The end of days!” The vicar cried. “The plagues are upon us. It’s the coming of the flood!” As he babbled, one of the monstrous toads leapt up and fastened itself to his thigh. As its needle-teeth embedded themselves deeply in the holy man’s flesh, he screamed in agony and pawed at his crucifix, desperately seeking salvation.

Before Moore and Poole could act, a swarm of toads fell upon the struggling vicar, snapping, snarling, chewing. The man’s screams were silenced with a sickening gurgle as one of the largest specimens sunk its fangs into his throat and tore.

“What are we going to do?” Poole shrieked.

“We have to find Sam. This must be his doing!” Moore asserted.

“What? The pie? But that’s just insane. You don’t really think that some mad-man has raised a toad-god, do you?” Poole babbled.

“Have you got a rational explanation for a plague of giant carnivorous toads?”

“Well, no.”

“Come along, then!” Moore barked.

“But where to? He could be anywhere!”

“Somewhere with a big oven!” Moore yelled after pondering for an instant.

“The Bakery!” Poole shouted in triumph, his face lighting up. It was his very own, personal, eureka moment.

The two men fled in the direction of the town bakery, kicking and dodging the toads as they went.

As they rounded the corner and the bakery came into view, the sky was lit with a gout of flame. The front window exploded, showering the sodden cobbles with shards of glass. Smoke billowed from the doorway, and the gambrel roof began to crack and sag.

"Now what?" Poole asked dryly.

IV.

The sleeping god is waking; nothing can stop Sam Francis now. Soon he will have all the knowledge, all the power, all the respect he deserves. The sleeping god is waking, and he is hungry. Once he has been given the magnificent pie, he will grant Sam Francis boons unimaginable. All he has to do is give him the pie and say the words. Nothing can go wrong now, nothing.

"Look; Over there." Poole points to what he initially thought was a sack of flour, but sacks of flour don't wriggle. "Someone's over there. He'll be burnt to a cinder if we don't do something."

Moore and Poole raced over, shielding their eyes from the flames. "Grab his legs!" Moore commanded and took the man's arms. "Now, drag him clear!" The two coppers dragged the wounded man to safety, seconds before a chunk of burning timber clattered to the very spot where he had lain.

Norman Travis, the local baker, was in a right old state. One of his arms had been burned quite badly.

The skin drooped like melted cheese. "That bastard!" He snarled through pain-gritted teeth. He was having trouble stopping his eyes from rolling due to the large dent in his forehead. "He came in and started chantin'. I told 'im to sling his hook, but he hit me on the head with my own bloody rollin' pin! Next thing I know, I'm wakin' up, and my bakery's on fire!"

"Any idea where he went?" Moore asked.

"He went off that way, towards the mud wallows, you know? The swamp down past the church, there's a path."

"Thanks, Norm. I'll send a quack as soon as I can. Oh, and keep away from the toads."

Moore and Poole raced off down the muddy path leaving the baker bewildered and bleeding. The toads had seemed to congregate in the town square. They smashed into businesses and ate whatever they could find.

The mud slopped and slurped as they pelted down the path. More checked his revolver and cursed. He had only one shot left, and it would have to do.

Below their pumping feet, the ground seemed to tremble and reverberate. Thunder cracked but didn't cease. It drew into one long, turgid, bowel-quaking rumble that seemed to coincide with the shaking of the earth.

Poole lost his footing on a fallen log and went spiralling into a bush. As Moore helped him to his feet, he heard a noise from just over the way. "Shhh," he whispered, bringing a finger sharply up to his lips. "I think I hear something."

Just past the bush that Poole had become intimately acquainted with was a clearing where three tributaries intersected. Sam Francis stood ankle-deep in the southernmost stream with his arms aloft and his head tilted back. On a large flat-topped rock, in a dry triangle in the centre of the flooding waters, sat the pie, golden and steaming.

Words were streaming from Sam's mouth. At least, Moore thought they were words. An insane babble of syllables, whoops, and howls. His eyes burned like hot coals, and his body trembled violently.

Moore burst from the bushes, his pistol levelled at the crazed youth's head. "Put your hands behind your head, and step away from the pie!" he bellowed.

"You're too late!" Sam chuckled, a wide, insane grin plastered across his pock-marked face. "He is waking!" His words trailed off into strange exultation as the ground shook even more wildly.

A monstrous splash from the stagnant pond beyond startled the two officers. Huge plumes of muddy water leapt into the sky. The water boiled, bubbled, and rose. It crashed over its banks and flowed toward town in a raging torrent.

Poole let out a startled cry of horror as a ghastly shape became visible. Two enormous wings stretched into the sky, taller than the tallest trees. They were attached to a colossal mound of blubber in the vague shape of a toad. Its skin was covered in thick bristly hairs, and it had what looked like bat ears.

"My lord!" Sam wailed in triumph, holding the pie in the air.

The toad-god licked its thick, rubbery lips with his leathery, bloated tongue. One large baleful eye opened and fixed on the pie. The beast sniffed the air. Thick globs of saliva dripped from its gaping maw and hit the water with a sizzle. It shifted its bulk in readiness for its tasty treat but was stopped short.

Moore squeezed the trigger on his Smith & Wesson, and the bullet cracked from the muzzle. It scythed through the air, narrowly missing Sam's head by a hair, and burst into the pie dish. Meat, gravy, pastry, and shards of Staffordshire pottery showered Sam.

The toad grumbled in anger at his spoiled tribute. Sam wailed and cried. "No!" he bellowed, "Lord Tsathoggua, eat those who defile your feast."

The toad seemed to think for a second. Its orange orbs surveyed the scene. Finally, its eyes came to rest on the one who woke him, Sam Francis.

"No, lord!" Sam cried in horror as the thick tongue of the toad whipped around his waist. His steak and kidney covered body was tossed into the air and swiftly dragged into the toad's gullet with a gulp.

The ground shook anew as the waters seemed to reverse back into the pond. A whirlpool opened, a portal to the muddy depths of the earth. The toad belched in appreciation of its meal and dived into the pool.

Moore and Poole stared in disbelief as a stampede of giant, toothy toads rushed from the town and followed their master to his world below.

Morning broke to a calm, sunny day. Many were dead at the teeth of the toads. None of the bodies remained, as the ravenous creatures had eaten every last morsel. A flood was blamed for the deaths. As far as the world knew, they were washed out to sea when the river burst its banks. The murders were officially listed as solved, and the flood was once again blamed for the absence of a corpse.

Moore, Poole, and all other witnesses and survivors were commended by the Queen herself and later bound to the Official Secrets Act.

The locals of Betyls Cove shun the site of the rising, Toad Rock, as it is now known. Nobody dares visit after dark.

The collection of books and papers found in Sam's house was turned over to Cambridge University, where it lies in the forbidden books library. All of Sam's diaries were burned and his recipe lost to time, thankfully. After all, as the sorcerer Eibon warned, it's best to just let sleeping toads lie.

⇛ **RECIPE** ⇚

'Tsathoggua's Tribute' Steak & Kidney Pie

1 Tablespoon beef dripping, lard, or cooking oil.
1 Lb stewing teak (chuck), diced.
1 Lb kidney, diced.
2 Lbs puff or shortcrust pastry.
1 Large onion, diced.
6 Scallions (spring onions), sliced.
2 Cloves of garlic, finely chopped.
1 Carrot, peeled and finely chopped.
1 Stick of celery, finely chopped.
1 Bottle of full-bodied red wine (Shiraz, Merlot, Zinfandel, etc.).
1 Bay leaf.
1 Tablespoon of finely chopped thyme.
Butter.
Worcestershire sauce.
Aged Balsamic Vinegar.
Salt.
Cracked black peppercorns.
Flour.
1 Egg (beaten).

Add a knob of butter to a small saucepan, and melt over a medium heat. Next, add the carrots, celery, and garlic. Sweat until soft. Remove from the heat, and set aside.

Place the steak and kidney into a bag or bowl.

Season with salt and black pepper, then add half of the thyme. Roll or shake the ingredients in flour, then add the contents to a sieve. Gently shake to remove any excess flour.

To a large pan, add the lard, onions, and scallions, and fry until soft. Add the meat and brown.

Next, add the rest of the thyme, the bay leaf, and the wine. Push the softened celery mix through a sieve and into the pot. Add a dash of balsamic vinegar and Worcestershire sauce, then bring to the boil.

Reduce the heat, and gently simmer for 90 minutes or until the sauce is reduced and thickened. The steak should be melt-in-the-maw tender. Take off the heat, cover, and allow to cool.

Pre-heat an oven to 220°C / 425°F

Roll out 2/3 of the pastry. It should be around a quarter of an inch thick and uniform. Line the interior of a well-greased pie dish. Leave an overhang of around an inch and a half.

Spoon the filling into the dish. Be sure to remove the bay leaf. Try to get the filling as even as possible.

Roll out the remaining pastry. Top the pie. Crimp and trim the edges.

Poke holes towards the centre of the pie to allow any steam to escape.

Glaze the pie with the beaten egg.

If you have any left-over pastry, why not cut some decorative shapes to garnish the pie? In this case, what about some evil, flesh-eating toads?

Place the pie in the centre of the pre-heated oven, and bake for 30-40 minutes, until golden.

Serve with mustard mashed potatoes and sautéed kale with black pepper, and you will have a meal fit for a gluttonous god.

The Birthday People

Don Raymond

For Katy Patchett

It was a summer rental, a small cottage lost amidst the thick milky fogs that crept and the small rains that fell upon an almost forgotten town somewhere on California's Lost Coast. No phone, no road, no forwarding address . . . and yet, despite all my efforts, the old bat had managed to find me.

"Yoo-hoo!" she ululated as she barged through the front door, the screen slamming shut with a metallic bang behind her. Her trilling soprano warbled down the hallway like a songbird—except she was free, and we were in the cage.

Angela whimpered and struggled to break free from my grip. I clamped a hand over her mouth and held her tighter. Her eyes were wide with panic, their whites clear even in the musty darkness of the bedroom closet. We crouched down below the level of the slats on the French doors, among boxes and bags still waiting to be unpacked, a cardboard corner pressing painfully into the soft flesh of my upper thigh.

"You know what day it is!" Aunt Edna taunted. I felt a wetness on my hand and looked down at Angela's tear-streaked face. She smiled for me, faking courage, and I loved her all the more because I could feel her heart racing even as she tried on the ill-fitting lie.

Edna puttered about the living room, rearranging knickknacks and generally making herself at home. She didn't need an invitation to go that far; after all, she was family.

I murmured, "Shhh," into Angela's ear, then gently kissed the top of her head. Without thinking, I rubbed her back; she started to scream, pulling hard away from me. I pressed my palm hard against her lips and held her more tightly, this time avoiding the spot between her shoulder blades where a red and angry wound still seeped blood. It had hurt me to cut into her, to bring such pain to my darling daughter, but necessity was mother also to cruelty, and with Edna even now stalking down the hallway, I knew I had been right.

Angela shuddered. "Hurts," she said.

Edna barked a short, canine laugh, the sound immense in the close silence. "All these calendars, Isaac! Was that all you could find? As if I'd let you forget your special day." She continued muttering to herself, her litany of endless self-conversation. "Personally, I've never liked to be reminded of time's passage. Tempus fugit and whatnot."

"If we just pretend we're not here, she'll go away," I whispered to Angela, smoothing her long hair. Even if Edna knew we were home—as she had to know, even though I'd parked back in town—it was still part of the ritual. The formalities had to be observed; it was our only chance.

A slight wavering of the light told me the bedroom door had opened, and Edna's footsteps stopped just on the threshold. A lighter flicked, and I smelled the sudden acrid pungency of tobacco. She would come no further. I relaxed, letting Angela slump against me, her tiny body soaking wet with terror.

"I talked to your mother the other day," Edna said. My breath caught in my chest in a sudden tight panic. "They should have the tests back any day. Oh, I do pray for her." She sighed, and in the aftersilence, the only sound was the crinkle of burning paper as she took a drag off her cigarette, narrow, thin, and pale—like her fingers, like her. "That poor woman. Time hasn't been kind to her."

I kicked the door open and rolled out into the air. Angela fell to her knees and crawled forward, gasping, a low moan torn from her belly. She drew her breath in fast, getting ready to scream.

"*There* you are!" Edna cried, clapping her hands together.

I sat on the floor, my legs splayed out before me, propping myself up on my hands. I knew how ridiculous I looked, but I was far beyond caring. "Come in," I muttered, and Edna moved into the room, kneeling next to me.

"Naughty boy. Hiding from your auntie on your birthday. Tsk tsk." She actually made the sound—tsk tsk—clucking with her tongue. She pressed her dry, dry lips to my cheek, a mummy's kiss, burning, dry as dust, and I was exhausted by even those minimal attentions. Her blue hair eclipsed my universe, the moon of her face drawing back to show her watery eyes, framed beneath octagonal glasses thick as leaded glass.

"Oh, and who's this?" she asked, turning to Angela, who scurried away from her touch, scampering like a rat across the floor. But Edna was there first, and Angela bumped into her varicose, control-stockinged legs. Edna bent down, surprisingly limber for an old woman, and raised one finger to Angela's chin, tilting her head up and turning her this way and that to frame her features in the light. Angela winced, whining through tight lips, but—paralyzed with fright - made no move to run.

Please, baby, just act normal, I thought at her. *Just be normal for a little bit . . . just until she's gone . . .*

"You never told us you had a baby girl!" Edna said. "Shame on you! Keeping such a beautiful creature from us! What's your name, love?"

"Angela," she whispered.

"Her mother and I, we . . . weren't speaking for a while," I said.

Edna flipped through her mental Rolodex, a memory of names and faces vaster than I could even begin to comprehend.

"Ka . . . ?" she ventured. "No. Clarissa, right? The redhead from Sunnyvale? The one who liked animals? Wasn't she going to become a vet?" She hadn't taken her hand from Angela.

"Clarissa," I agreed. "She's . . . not well right now."

Edna let one finger trail along Angela's cheek. Almost, there was a spark of recognition in her eyes.

She tilted her head, and I was struck by how birdlike she was: thin, inquisitive, hungry.

I'd cut the wards well. After a last, lingering touch, she released Angela's chin, and with only a brief final look, she rose to her feet, offering her hand to me.

"Well, come along, dear," she said, "we've a birthday to celebrate."

She lifted me seemingly without effort, and I trailed behind her as she waltzed into the living room, singing *"Happy Birthday"* as she twirled like an excited young girl. She handed me a box, excruciatingly precision wrapped with iridescent pink and mother-of-pearl wrapping interspersed with desperately cheerless little multi-colored dots.

"It's so dark and gloomy in here. I swear, you'll all die of mold. We need light! We need air! It's a party, after all!" She threw the curtains aside, and both Angela and I winced back from the sudden radiance. Edna wallowed in the thin oceanic sunlight, warming her old bones.

"Ooh, I never get tired of that," she said. "Here, I'll make us some tea."

She wandered into the kitchen, producing a cinnamon-scented aluminum canister from the mysterious, voluminous confines of her purse. I knelt down and caught Angela's eye.

"Go hide in your room, and don't come out until I tell you, okay? No matter what you hear."

"Hungry," she said.

"I know. We'll eat when she's gone. Can you do this for me, please? Can you do this for daddy?"

With a quick, bobbing nod, she turned and ran on silent bare feet to her room, peering out from behind the door until she heard Edna returning. With a final click, she locked herself in.

Edna handed me a cup of henna tea on an antique saucer. The smell—turmeric and clove—took me back to my childhood, to what had felt then like one long summer day. The tea was soothing: thick and sweet and just a little smoky. I could think of nothing better in this world. I set it on the table.

"Drink," she insisted, taking a seat on the couch. She sipped, the wattles under her neck shaking as she swallowed, then sat, humming to herself. "I remember when I used to have birthdays," she said after a moment.

"Doesn't everyone have birthdays?" I asked, even though I'd heard the joke before.

"Oh, no, I gave them up long ago. Now I just celebrate their anniversaries," she said.

I laughed dutifully and decided I needed the tea after all. I took a sip, then reached for my present. She batted my hand away coquettishly.

"We can't have presents without cake!" she said, rising. "Don't tell me you forgot cake, too! Honestly, Isaac, has being a father rattled your brain?"

"No one told me it would be this hard," I said.

"I'm always willing to help, Isaac. All you have to do is ask."

"I'm just . . . so tired, all the time. It's stretched my budget to rent this place, but Angela needed some time away. She doesn't do well with people, just yet." I went into the kitchen, made a show of rattling cupboards. I came out with my creation, made especially for this day, a black, doughy cake, unfrosted, looking almost like a banana bread. The sugar glaze glistened, sticky and translucent in the watery sun, and it was speckled with bits of fire-engine red and orange, with darker blotches of raisins, dates, prunes, and heavy with thick alcoholic syrup. It was cool from the refrigerator, but the barest scent of tart fruit came from it, a bit of spring's exuberance meant for winter's long dark.

"Will this do?" I asked, setting the platter down on the table and backing away, raising my arms as if presenting an offering.

Edna arched one perfectly drawn eyebrow. "A fruitcake?"

I forced a smile.

"Actually, it's Emily Dickinson's black cake." I paused.

Silence.

"Okay, it's a fruitcake. I'm stuck on my thesis. What am I supposed to say about Emily Dickinson that hasn't already been said? So I thought about looking at other aspects of her life. Did you know she was an accomplished baker?"

"I suppose, sitting around all day like that, she had the time."

"Oh, but that's just it. She might not have got out much, but she was hardly a hermit. Her recipes use coconut, rum, and ginger; she wrote poetry on the back of a Parisian chocolate wrapper. Even a recluse in a little town in Massachusetts in the 19th century had access to food from all over the world.

"I wonder, if we'd lived back then, if we would have known her mostly for her cooking? Most of her poetry wasn't published until after her death. It makes you wonder about the secrets people keep."

Some of her mimsy disregard left her, then, as if she sensed, perhaps, the lurking of plots beneath her awareness. But the ritual was in motion, and she could not refuse. There had to be cake, an offering of bread, and within those circuits, she was as bound as I.

"It's good to see you so excited about something for a change, Isaac! Hopefully, you'll get that thesis done. I want to read it first, of course." She raised her fork in mock salute. "I suppose, since we're celebrating, we can make do," she said, holding out a saucer.   I sawed through the dough, making sure she got a generous helping of fruit. I set it on her plate, then cut a smaller piece for me.

She smiled, a thin-lipped simper that didn't reach her eyes. "Oh no, dear, that's far too much for me. Why don't we switch?" She placed her plate in front of me, taking mine. She sat, slowly tapping her fork against the spongy dough. "Doesn't Angela want any?"

"She has a nut allergy. Maybe gluten, too."

She nodded and took a small bite with her front teeth, delicately cutting off a tiny square with infinite precision. She chewed methodically, wetting the dough with tea until it formed a mushy paste in her mouth, then swallowed.

"So are you making any progress, then? How many units do you have left?"

"Too many. Time got away from me this year. Just like last year and the one before."

"It does that when you have children. Or so I'm told," she said with a wink. She pointed to the blue-and-white porcelain cake platter. "I made that, you know. For your mother. I thought it would cheer her up. I tried to get her to go to my ceramics class, but she was too busy with you.”

“Honestly, when I think about how much I have left to do, it’s like a tidal wave. I just feel drowned under the weight of it, and I get so tired just thinking about it. It’s been so long, and . . . ”

She leaned forward encouragingly, and I sighed.

“Mom’s so far gone, I don’t know that it would mean anything anymore. She’s the one who fought for me to go to school, and now it’s too late to vindicate her.”

She handed my box to me. “Here, dear, open your present.”

My muscles obeyed her automatically. I tore the paper away, revealing-

“A shirt and tie?” I said. “Thanks, I guess, but— Aunt Edna, I’m not really the tie type.”

“I know, you dress like a farmer,” she said, plucking at my shirt. “But it’s time you started moving up in the world. You have an interview next Tuesday with an old friend of mine. He’s got a spot open in his accounting department. I told him you’d be perfect for it, even without a degree.”

“Your friends can be very pliable.”

She smiled. “Of course. I can be very persuasive when I need to. But don’t worry, I’m not throwing you to the sharks. I think you’ll do quite nicely there.”

“An office job. Do you know, that’s the one thing I never wanted? Mom would be so proud.” I leaned back on the couch, gazing into time’s horizon.

“Poetry doesn’t pay the bills, dear. You have a child to take care of now.”

"*Between the motion / And the act / Falls the shadow,*" I said. "Always in the stillness of the year, you came."

"Well, your birthday's in August . . . "

"But never Thanksgiving, never Christmas. Never just to visit. Just my birthday."

"You were just a child, dear. I doubt you even remember all the times I visited your mother. I'd come now, too, if you ever bothered to put up a tree."

"Oh, I remember quite well. At first, I looked forward to it, you know? Not just the presents, but growing up. I barely knew you then, but every time you came, it seemed like a little more of the world opened up. The pencil mark on the kitchen wall was a little higher. My allowance increased, I knew more words. Everything good seemed to be destined for me.

"But it never actually happened. There was never a destination; I just kept getting older. Each year, it was harder to get up in the morning, a little less worth the effort to try. Too tired to go to class. To take chances. And finally, I just . . . gave up, let the world do with me what it wanted.

"So thanks, Aunt Edna. For everything." I'd never dared raise my voice to her before. I braced myself, sitting on the edge of the love seat, uncertain what would come next.

To my surprise, she laughed and sipped her tea. "Oh, that wasn't me, dear, it was your uncle. He always was greedy." The saucer tinkled as she set the cup down. "But then, he needed you more. He was older than me. He wasn't strong enough to make it, that year you hid yourself away."

"Don't call him my uncle."

"Well, what should I call him, then?" A faint wisp of irritation from her. Her hand clenched, just momentarily—but I noticed, and she noticed me noticing.

"For so long, I didn't understand," I said.

"Understand what, dear?" She finished her cake, her eyes tracking me as I slowly ate each piece. She picked up her tea again, holding the saucer, not setting it down on the table, the way old women drink tea.

You've learned to mimic us so very well . . .

"I went to his house, you know. When he died."

There was a faint whisper of—what? Dread? Curiosity in her eyes? "Oh?"

"I didn't understand most of what I found . . . it took a long time to find somebody to help me. There aren't many who can read Ugarit these days."

"It's Ugr'tis, dear," she said. She patted my knee. "I know, it's hard without the vowels."

"So what do I call you? Pazzuzu? Pazzizil? Azazel?"

"I always thought *lilitu* had a certain poetry to it. But you can just call us the Birthday People."

"How old *are* you?"

"Oh, it's so hard to keep up with all the different dating systems. Last time I checked, it was somewhere around six thousand or so years."

I knew, vaguely, but it was still shocking to hear her say it. I shook my head. "I can't even imagine that much time."

She set her saucer down, at last, a little of the amber liquid splashing over the rim. "I can't imagine any less. So much to do . . . do you know, there's half a world I haven't even seen yet?" She chuckled. "Time's like a city. No matter how big it gets, you end up living in the same small circle of your neighborhood, going to the same stores, eating at the same places. And there's always someone for a knitting circle or needing a pottery class or another for bunco."

"I . . . bunco?!?"

She nodded. "Of course, back then, the dice were made of bone." She closed her eyes and smiled. "They made such a lovely rattling sound. Oh, not human bone, of course. Sheep, mostly. We weren't monsters, after all."

"What's your name? Your real name, I mean."

She blinked. "Edna, dear. You know that."

I waited.

"Fine. I am called as Enheduanna, high priestess of Inanna. You know her as Lilith. Does this knowledge bring you happiness?"

"I gave up on happiness long ago."

"That's a shame. It makes me said when the people I love aren't happy."

"I wouldn't even be here if it weren't for Angela."

"Angela," she said, savoring the name like a morsel. "She'll be taking all of your time now, you know. That's how children are."

"Better her than you."

She pouted. "I'm hurt. After all I've done for you."

"Too bad you didn't have children of your own. Someone to waste all of that endless prying energy on."

"But then I never would have had the pleasure of knowing you. Or your lovely Angela. Oh, I just know we're going to be such good friends! Tell me all about her."

Her mouth twitched, just a little, what I might have taken for a facial tick if I hadn't been raised by that face; I knew her every wrinkle. Almost time.

"Her mother was with me," I said, "when I went to his house."

"Your uncle's. It was unwise of you to go. I can see how it might have confused you." Her hand crept toward my chin, but she frowned suddenly and pulled it back, reaching instead for her alligator skin purse, which she set in her lap, clutching it in both hands. It reminded me of a lap dog.

"It did something to her. She left after that. Took Angela with her." I couldn't help keeping the anger from my voice. "I don't know what happened to her. Something bad, I'm sure. I don't think Angela had much of a childhood. I'm all she's got now. Maybe all she'll ever have. She's half feral."

"Oh!" Edna said, then "oh," as she realized what she'd felt earlier in the bedroom. Too casually, she tried to light a cigarette. The lighter fell to the carpet with a muffled thump, followed shortly by her capsizing purse as she tried and failed to stand. Her knees buckled beneath her, and she crumpled to the floor, catching herself on the table's edge.

"What did you do?" she asked as her face turned even paler.

"Extract of belladonna."

"Deadly nightshade!" she cried.

"In the dates, so the fiber would slow it down. I figured your system would detect it otherwise. And poison dates seemed . . . oh, poetic, I guess."

"But you . . . "

I nodded. It took both hands to stand, and my knees were water. I was shaking, but I didn't know if it was the poison or bottled years of anger finally bursting forth.

"Oh, yes. But the cattle are so big and dumb. Healthy stock, Edna. I only need to live long enough to deal with you."

She chuckled, though all that came was a wheeze. She murmured something in an ancient language, then met my eyes. A slow, chalk smile. "It will take more than nightshade for that, Dumuzi. But you . . . you had so many delicious years left in you." She shook her head, looking at me with hungry sorrow. She licked her lips, once, with the tip of her tongue, and coughed.

My legs gave out, and I fell beside her. I reached one lead arm to where she lay, haloed by ash and cosmetics, face powders staining the rug all the colors she could never be. "Maybe," I said, "but one myth is true, though."

"Which one, little shepherd?"

"Running water," was all I could manage.

She screeched and kicked away from me, flapping her arms like a bat, clutching at the table. I captured her flailing hands and dragged her down the hall, kicking my feet along the rug to gain traction.

God, she was strong! She got one claw around a corner and clung like a drowning rat.

"Angela! It's time, baby! Turn on the shower!"

I pulled and pulled, trying to break Edna's grip as she screamed.

"Please! Please! Ah, someone help me!"

Angela poked her head out of the bedroom, then scurried down the hall; a moment later, the static hiss of water echoed from the bathroom.

I kicked at Edna's hand until I heard bones snap. She groaned and clutched her fingers to her, and I pulled her farther along. With a snarl, she wrapped her working fingers around my ankle, clawing at my leg. Her talons tore my pants, gouging burning trails of fire down my calf.

"Nothing without me!" she hissed. "After all I did for you! Ah! Help!"

I saved my energy for dragging. We were almost there. Angela stood, silent, staring at us from the hallway, her hands hung loosely at her sides, head tilted.

Edna left a trail of blood and skin and falling hair behind her. Beneath my grip, she flopped about the floor, twisting left and right, trying to break free, her legs kicking futilely behind her. One shoe came off, and I saw her nails cut through her stockings to dig into the fiber of the carpet. I kicked her head, and she shivered, seized, and ceased resisting.

There! I felt cool tile beneath me. The mist from the shower enveloped us, and with a final effort, I heaved both of us into the tub.

Edna shrieked like a tea kettle, her makeup sloughing off in suddenly slimy sheets, revealing leathery skin shrink-wrapped to a skeleton, a few wispy hairs all that remained of her humanity. She struggled to claw her way out of the tub, her talons scrabbling for purchase on the white, pristine porcelain. Her eyes, disconcertingly huge in that gaunt face, narrowed with hate as she caught my gaze.

I averted my eyes, and she lashed out with an elbow, catching me in the solar plexus, and what little breath I had left escaped me. My mouth opened and closed, but neither air nor words came through. My heart thundered and slowed, and the purple curtains began to close. My strength gave out, and my grip broke. Edna shrugged free of my embrace and rolled out of the tub.

"Oh, almost, dear," she said, as she stood on wobbly feet, a black shadow in my fading vision. "A moment more, and you might have had me, Dumuzi. But you never could have truly hoped to stand against me."

Angela stepped silently into the room behind her.

By the time Edna turned her back to me, it was already too late. Moving faster than I could follow, Angela pounced on the old woman, bearing her down amidst screams and flailing. She kissed Edna on her cheeks, her eyelids, and the top of her leathery head. She ran her hands over Edna's naked, squamous scalp, and clutched that withered face to her chest as if nursing her. With each unasked-for caress, Edna's struggles grew weaker. Finally, her shrieks stopped as she crumpled to dust beneath Angela's hands.

Angela fell to her knees, shaking and moaning, clutching at her sides as her breasts and hips swelled, taking on the fullness of young womanhood. She coughed, spitting up bits of Edna's skin, and ran her hands down her body, staring in disbelief. With each burst of growth, she grew taller and thinner until, splayed against the tub, one skinny arm hanging over the edge, she looked at me with the hollow cheeks and hungry sunken eyes of an addict.

I was shivering, from more than just the cold.

Angela whined, a high, inhuman sound. "I'm hungry," she hissed through a rictus grin.

With what strength I had, I held up my arm to her. She lifted me, cradling my head, stroking and kissing me, murmuring "daddy" over and over, and what years I had left flowed from me to her, my dearest darling daughter, my birthday girl.

Emily Dickinson's Black Cake

1 1/4 lbs of dark raisins

10 oz of currants

6 oz (1 cup) of finely-diced citron

1/4 cup of all-purpose flour (spooned into the cup and leveled)

2 cups (8 ounces) of sifted unbleached all-purpose flour

1/2 tsp of salt

1/4 tsp of baking soda

1 tsp of freshly grated nutmeg

1/2 tsp of ground cinnamon

1/4 tsp of ground cloves

1/2 lb (2 sticks) of unsalted butter, at room temperature

1 cup of granulated sugar

4 large eggs

1/4 cup of brandy

1/4 cup molasses

Adjust two oven racks with one in the center and one in the lowest position. Preheat the oven to 250°F. Butter two 8 1/2 x 4 1/2 x 2 3/4 inch loaf pans. Line the bottoms of the pans with parchment or waxed paper cut to fit, and butter the paper.

Set the pans aside. Place a 13 x 9 x 2 inch pan half-filled with hot tap water on the lower oven rack.

In a large bowl combine the raisins, currants, and citron. Add the 1/4 cup of flour and toss the fruits to coat. Set aside.

Whisk together in a medium bowl the 2 cups of flour with the salt, nutmeg, cinnamon, and cloves. Beat the butter with the paddle attachment of an electric stand mixer on medium speed until very soft and smooth, about 1 minute. While beating on medium speed, gradually sprinkle in the sugar, 2 to 3 tablespoons at a time, and beat for about 20 seconds between additions. When all the sugar has been added, scrape the bowl and beater and beat on medium-high uninterrupted for 5 minutes. In a 2-cup glass measure or small bowl, beat the eggs with a fork just to combine the yolks and whites.

While beating on low speed, drizzle in the eggs in 2 to 3 tablespoon installments. Beat until each addition is thoroughly incorporated before adding the next. The batter may look curdled; don't be concerned. When all the eggs are in, scrape the bowl and beat on medium high speed for 3 minutes. At this point the batter should be smooth and fluffy. Scrape the bowl and beater well.

With the machine on low speed, alternately add the sifted dry ingredients in 3 additions and the brandy in 2 additions, beginning and ending with the dry ingredients. Beat only until each addition is thoroughly incorporated. Add the molasses and beat it in on low speed. Transfer the batter to a large, wide, shallow bowl with about an 8-quart capacity (mine is 13 1/2 inches in diameter and 4 3/4 inches deep). For ease in mixing, it is important that the bowl not be too deep.

Now you will add the fruit to the batter, but it must be done gradually. In the play, "The Belle of Amherst," Miss Dickinson says "slowly now—as you stir." Scatter a handful of the fruits over the batter and stir them in well with a wooden spoon. Stir until each piece is well-coated with batter. Continue adding the fruits a handful at a time, making sure to stir until well-coated with the batter before adding the next installment. If you add the fruits too fast, they will tend to stick together in clumps instead of remaining in separate pieces. The batter will be very stiff once all the fruits are in. Spoon the batter into the pans, packing it down with a rubber spatula to remove any air pockets. The pans will be about three-fourths full. Place the pans in the oven on the middle rack.

After 2 hours of baking remove the pan of water. Continue baking the cakes for another 1 to 1 1/2 hours, until they spring back when gently pressed and a thin wooden skewer inserted into the centers comes out clean. Total baking time is 3 to 3 1/2 hours.

Place the cake pans on a wire rack and cool the cakes completely. Run a thin-bladed sharp knife around the edges of the cakes to release them and invert the pans onto a counter top. If the cakes don't fall out right away, rap the pans sharply on the counter to release the cakes. Lift off the pans, and peel the papers off the cakes. Wrap each cake in plastic wrap, and then in foil, and refrigerate them. This cake is far easier to cut when cold. Place the cake with its bottom side up on a cutting board, and cut into thin slices using a sharp serrated knife. If you want your cakes to have a little kick, brush them with a spoonful or two of brandy or rum before wrapping them up.

The cakes will keep for up to 6 weeks in the refrigerator, or they may be frozen for 4 to 6 months.
Makes 2 loaves.

About the Contributors

Michael Allen Rose is a Chicago based author, musician and performer. He has published several bizarro, horror and comic novels with various presses, been in a few anthologies, and also makes industrial music under the name Flood Damage. He has a Patreon which provides subscribers with a new zine or chapbook every month. He loves cats, good tea, great food, and his partner Sauda with whom he poses nude for art classes and performs burlesque with for money, not unlike some kind of poorly trained monkey. He is the host of the Ultimate Bizarro Showdown each year at Bizarro Con in Portland, Oregon, and is involved in many shenanigans. Find out more at www.gerbilprobe.com

Karen Heslop writes from Kingston, Jamaica. Her stories can be found in *The Weird and Whatnot, Haunted MTL* and *AHF Magazine* among others.

Joel Murray is a software test engineer by day and aspiring horror author, songwriter, and drummer by night. "Sweet Tooth" is his first published work. Joel lives in Nashville with his wonderful wife Loee and their sassy terrier Finn. As you read this, Joel is most likely eating too much peanut butter and planning next year's Halloween costume.

Kristi Petersen Schoonover is not a fan of sauerbraten, although she was forced to eat it many times as a kid. Her work has appeared in many magazines and anthologies, and she's the author of the collection *The Shadows Behind*. She was the recipient of three Norman Mailer Writers Colony Residencies and holds an MFA in Creative Writing from Goddard College. She serves as a co-host of the *Dark Discussions* podcast, as founding editor of the dark literary journal *34 Orchard*, and lives in the Connecticut woods with her husband, Nathan. Follow her adventures at kristipetersenschoonover.com.

D.M. Slate resides in Colorado and enjoys spending time outdoors with her family. Slate has been writing dark fiction for over a decade and enjoys shocking her readers with the unexpected. More information can be found at her website: www.dm-slate.com.

Kate Tyte was born in Bath, England, studied English literature and worked as an archivist for ten years. She now lives in Lisbon where she is an English teacher. She is a regular contributor of literary essays to *Slightly Foxed* magazine and her short stories have been published in *Storgy, Riggwelter* and *The Fiction Pool*. She is a book reviewer for *Storgy* and *The Short Story*.

Nidheesh Samant is a marketing professional from India. He enjoys dark tales and is obsessed with soup. He hopes to become a best selling author of riveting thrillers. Nidheesh blogs at thedarknetizen.wordpress.com

Tim Mendees was born in Macclesfield in the North-West of England. He has recently been published in *Death and Butterflies (suicide House Publishing,) Solitude (DBND Publishing,)* and has had several short stories accepted for publication in forthcoming anthologies and magazines. His debut novella, *Miracle Growth,* is set to be released later in 2020.
https://www.facebook.com/goatinthemachine

Originally hailing from the backwaters of San Jose, **Don Raymond** now lives in the tiny hamlet of Alturas, California, where he works as an accountant at the local casino, which is not a career path his counselors ever mentioned to him. He spends his free time mediating the Machiavellian feline politics of his neighborhood. You can read more of his work at *Martian Migraine Press, Bone & Ink Press,* and *Bourbon Penn.* He also once didn't make a left turn at Albuquerque.

Erin Reynolds graduated from the U.S. Coast Guard Academy and began her career patrolling the Caribbean. Erin currently works as an Emergency Management Specialist, writing and editing contingency plans and exercises, and as an editor for Madness Heart Press. Erin watched her first horror film *Deep Blue Sea* at the age of 4, and has enjoyed being terrified ever since. Erin lives in Puerto Rico with her husband and two dogs.